PUSHKIN PRESS

THE BACHELORS

ADALBERT STIFTER (1805–1868) was an Austrian writer, painter and poet closely associated with the Biedermeier movement in European art. Following his studies at the University of Vienna, he worked as a tutor for aristocratic families before becoming a supervisor of elementary schools. He is particularly renowned for the vivid descriptions of natural landscapes in his writing, and has been celebrated by both German and English writers including Rainer Maria Rilke, Thomas Mann, W.G. Sebald, W.H. Auden and Hermann Hesse.

D0901365

ADALBERT STIFTER

THE BACHELORS

Translated from the German by
David Bryer

PUSHKIN PRESS
LONDON

Pushkin Press
71–75 Shelton Street
London WC2H 9JQ

English translation © David Bryer 2008

The Bachelors was first published in this version in 1850 as *Der Hagestolz*

First published by Pushkin Press in 2008
This edition first published in 2019

The translation of this book was supported by the
Austrian Federal Ministry of Education, Arts and Culture

1 3 5 7 9 8 6 4 2

ISBN 13: 978-1-78227-607-4

Offset by Tetragon, London
Printed and bound by CPI Group (UK) Ltd, Croydon, CRO 4YY

www.pushkinpress.com

THE BACHELORS

I

CHALK AND CHEESE

ON A BEAUTIFUL GREEN hill-slope, where trees grew and nightingales sang, several young men were frolicking and cavorting, as young men do who stand but barely on the threshold of their lives. A dazzling landscape spread out all around them. The shadows of clouds flitted across, and looking up from down below on the plain were the towers and clusters of houses of a large town.

One of these youths cried out: "One thing is now absolutely certain, today and forever—I'll never marry."

The one who said this was a slim lad with soft, wistful eyes. The others paid this scant attention; several laughed, broke off branches, hurled them at each other and continued on their way.

"Hey, who's going to get married, anyway," one of them said, "tied to the stupid apron-strings of a woman and sitting perched like a bird in a cage?"

"All right, you idiot, but what about dancing, falling in love, getting embarrassed and going red in the face, eh?" shouted another, and again laughter rang out.

"No girl would have you anyway."

"Nor you."

"So what?"

The next words could no longer be heard. Boisterous shouts came back from amidst the tree trunks and then nothing, for the young men were already going up the steep stretch that led away and up from the clearing, as could be seen from the swaying of the bushes. They strode energetically forwards in the dazzling sunlight; all around them the branches were coming into leaf, and on their cheeks and in their eyes shone a total and unshakable confidence in the world. Round about them lay Spring, as inexperienced and confident as they. The young man who had spoken of his decision not to wed had said nothing more on the subject and it had been forgotten.

A fresh burst of chatter and lively exchange flowed from their ready tongues. They talked first about everything, and often all at the same time. Then they talked of the loftiest things, and next of the most profound, quickly exhausting both subjects. Then it's the turn of state affairs. Boundless freedom, justice of the highest order and the most limitless tolerance are to reign in the land, such is the recommendation. Whoever is opposed to this will be struck down and brought to heel. The country's foes must be annihilated and then round the brows of the heroes glory will shine forth. While they were speaking of—in their opinion—great things, around about them only little things—also in their opinion—were happening: everywhere the bushes were turning green, the brooding earth was germinating and beginning to play with her first little Spring creatures, as one might with jewels.

After this they sing a song, then chase each other, push each other into the ditch or the bushes, cut switches and sticks, and in the process climb ever higher up the hillside and above the dwelling-places of men.

We must remark at this point what a puzzling, indescribable, mysterious and fascinating thing the future is, before it becomes our present—and when it has, how quickly it rushes by, slipping through our fingers—and then how delineated it lies there as the past, spent and insubstantial! All these young men are storming their way into this future, seemingly unable to wait for it. One of them boasts of things and of pleasures above his years, the other affects an ennui, as if he had already drained life to the dregs, while the third parrots expressions heard at his father's house from the lips of older men and grey-beards. Then they snatch at a passing butterfly and find a brightly coloured stone on the path.

They toil on up ever higher and higher. Up by the edge of the wood they look back down at the town. Of all the various houses and buildings they can see, they take bets as to which ones are which. Then they press on into the shadows of the beeches.

The ground is almost level in the wood. Once out of it, however, bright meadows planted with fruit trees drop down into a valley that quietly and secretly winds around the overarching mountains, down from which tumble two sparkling, glassy streams. The waters ripple happily over the polished pebbles past thickly-growing orchards, garden fences and houses, and from there back into the vineyards. And all this is so quiet that often the crowing of the cock or the single stroke of the church tower bell can be heard carried on the clear afternoon breeze. The valley is seldom visited by townsfolk and none has yet erected their summer holiday house there.

Our friends, however, run rather than walk across and down the meadow into this gently suspended cradle of a valley. Noisily they descend to the garden allotments, cross the first plank bridge, then the second, walk alongside the water's edge and finally barge their way into a garden abounding in elder, nut and lime trees. It is the garden of an inn-house. Here they cluster round one of the tables, its legs like all the others hidden in grass, with their nailed-down tops on which are displayed carved hearts and the names of those who had sat at the table long before. Each of them ordered what he wanted for lunch. When they had downed this, they played for a while with a poodle that was in the garden, paid the bill and then headed off. They walked through the entrance of the valley and into a broader one where a river flowed. On reaching this, they took a small boat that was moored up and, in their naivety, rowed across to a spot known to be dangerous. Women who happened to be passing were horrified when they saw the young people rowing there. On the other side of the river they hired a man to row the boat back again and tie it up at the place from where they had taken it.

Then they pressed on through reed-covered water-meadows until they reached a causeway over which a road ran and where a tavern stood. They hired an open carriage from the landlord in order to drive back into town along what was now the opposite side of the river. They flew past meadows, thickets, fields, public parks, gardens and houses until they reached the fringes of town, where they got out. On their arrival the sun, which had been such a friendly companion to them the whole day, was hanging like a glowing, fading ball on the far horizon. When it had set, the hills on which they had sported in the morning looked to the friends like a plain blue band rising up against the yellow evening sky.

They then walked towards the town and its dusty streets now fading into dusk. At a certain place they went their separate ways, bidding each other loud and cheerful fare-wells.

"Goodbye," said one.

"Goodbye," replied the other.

"Goodnight—my greetings to Rosina."

"Goodnight—my greetings to August and Theobald tomorrow."

"And mine to Karl and Lothar."

More names were mentioned, for the young have many friends and every day new ones knock on the door. They parted. Two of them took the selfsame way and the one said to the other: "Now you can stay the night at my place, Victor, and leave tomorrow as early as you like—Is it really true that you don't want to marry?"

"I tell you straight," replied the young man he had addressed, "I most definitely won't marry and that I'm very unhappy."

But his eyes were so bright when he said this and the lips so young over which these words lightly passed.

The two friends walked along the street a little further and then turned into a familiar house, up two floors and past rooms filled with lights and people.

They came into a solitary room.

"There, Victor," said the other, "I've had a bed set up next to mine, so that you can have a good night's rest. My sister Rosina will send us up some food—we can stay here and enjoy ourselves. That was a heavenly day and I really don't want to spend the last part of it in company. I've already told Mother that—is that all right with you, Victor?"

"Of course," he answered, "it's very boring at your father's table when there's such a long delay between courses, during which he holds forth so much. But tomorrow, Ferdinand, there's no two ways about it but I must be off at first light."

"As soon as you want," replied Ferdinand. "You know where the house-key is kept, hung up inside that recess in the entrance."

During this conversation they began to undress and take off their cumbersome, dirty boots. One item of clothing was put here, another there. A servant brought lights and a maid a dinner tray generously laden with food. They bolted it all down indiscriminately. Then they looked out first of the one then the other window, walked around the room, examined the presents that Ferdinand had received only the day before, counted the red sunset clouds, undressed fully and got into bed, where they continued talking, but before long neither of them was capable either of talking or thinking, as they were both fast asleep.

The same may have been the case with the others who had shared with them the day's same pleasures.

While these young lads had been enjoying this day in such a way, something different had been happening in another place. An old man had spent the day sitting in the sun on the bench in front of his house. Far from the green, wooded spot where the nightingales sang and where the young men had laughed so happily, and behind the shining blue mountains that bordered the view, there lay an island on which this house stood. The old man sat by the house and trembled at the thought of dying. You might have been able to see him sitting there for many years now, in the unlikely event of his granting anyone permission to look at him there. Since he had never married, no old female companion had sat with him that day on the bench, nor in all the other places he may have been before he acquired his island house; never had he had the company of a wife. He had never had children, never been pestered or delighted by them, and so none hovered there in the shadow he cast from the bench onto the sand. It was very silent in the house and, whenever he chanced to go in, he locked the door himself, and whenever he came out, it was he again who opened it. While the youngsters had been toiling up their hillside surrounded by teeming life and intense happiness, he had been sitting on his bench, looking at the spring flowers tied to their stakes, and the barren air and the sunlight had played vainly about him. When, at the end of the day, the youngsters had collapsed into bed and were sunk in slumber, he, too, was lying in bed in a well-guarded room and squeezing his eyes shut in order to get to sleep.

And so it was that, under its cool mantle of stars, this same night descended, indifferent as to whether there were young hearts who rejoiced at the day gone by, without having ever given one thought to death as if it didn't exist, or as to whether there was an old man who lived in fear of a violent shortening of his life and who, however, was once again one day nearer that moment.

II

HARMONY

WHEN THE NEXT DAY'S first pale light began to dawn, Victor was already on his way, his footsteps echoing in the still deserted streets of the town. There was not a soul to be seen at first; then he started to encounter many a grumpy, half-asleep figure, obliged to begin work early, while the distant but growing rattle of carts signalled the first deliveries of provisions to the large and needy town. He made his way to the town gates. Once through these he was greeted by the cool and damp green of the fields. The first sliver of the sun was showing at the edge of the world and the tips of the wet grass were afire with green and red. The larks were warbling joyfully in the air, while the nearby town, normally so noisy, was still almost completely silent.

When he felt he was well beyond the walls of the town, he immediately struck a course through the fields towards that green and wooded spot of which we have already spoken, where the day before the nightingales had been singing and the young men had been gallivanting about. This he reached after walking for nearly two hours. From there he took the same route as he had the day before with his friends. He climbed the steep hillside with the bushes, without looking about him, pressed on under the trees, hurried on and then climbed down through the meadow with the fruit trees into the valley earlier described as so quiet and where the two sparkling streams flowed.

When he reached the bottom of the valley, he crossed the first bridge; only today, as if in greeting, he looked down for a while at the shiny pebbles over which the water was rippling. Then he crossed the second bridge and walked along by the water. But today he didn't go as far as the inn-house garden where they had eaten the day before but turned off much earlier at a place where a large elder bush stood dangling its branches and roots in the water. There he left the path and walked in among the elders and bushes. There was a garden fence, which had acquired its ash-grey colour from countless bouts of rain and sunshine, and in this fence there was a little gate. Victor opened this and went in. Here there was a garden and, a little way off, the long white wall of a low house, against which elder bushes and fruit trees stood out in relief. The house had sparkling clean windows and, behind these, white curtains were hanging peacefully.

Victor walked along the edge of the bushes towards the house. When he had reached the sandy clearing in front of the house, on which stood the well and an ancient apple tree, against which stakes and a variety of other things were leaning, he was greeted with lots of tail-wagging by an old Pomeranian dog. The house's other neighbours, some equally cheerful chickens, continued scratching unperturbed under the apple-tree. He entered the house, crunching across the sand of the entrance hall and into the living-room, in which there was a clean, polished floor.

Alone in the room was an old woman, who had just opened a window and was busy wiping down the white-washed tables, chairs and cupboards, and re-arranging things that had probably got out of place the evening before. Distracted from her work by the sound of the young man coming in, she turned her face towards him, the face of an old but beautiful woman, something so rarely seen. Its various pastel shades of colour were soft and each one of the countless little wrinkles bespoke kindliness and warmth. Around all these wrinkles were the further innumerable wrinkles of a snow-white, crimped bonnet. On each cheek there was a delicate blush of red.

"There you are already, Victor," she said. "I've forgotten to keep the milk warm again. Everything's by the fire, but that will have gone out. If you wait, I'll get it going again with the billows."

"I'm not hungry, Mother," said Victor. "Before I set off from Ferdinand's, I ate two cold slices of what was left over from supper last night."

"But you must be hungry," replied the woman. "You've been walking for four hours in the morning air and then through the damp woods."

"It's not that far over the meadows."

"Yes, because you always think while you're walking that your feet will hold out forever—but they don't—and you don't notice how tired you're getting—but once you've sat down for a while, then your feet will hurt."

She didn't say anything further but went out into the kitchen. Victor, meanwhile, sat down on a chair.

When she came in again she said, "Are you tired?"

"No," he replied.

"You soon will be. Dog-tired. Wait a bit—everything will be warmed through in a moment."

Victor gave no reply but, bending down low towards the dog, which had come in with him, he stroked its soft, long fur with the flat of his hand. The animal responded equally affectionately by sitting upright and was now fixedly gazing into his eyes. He was stroking it in the same place and looking at this same place all the time, as if his heart was deeply moved.

The old woman continued meanwhile with her housework. She was very diligent. Whenever she couldn't reach the dust, she would go on tiptoe in order to remove the unwelcome visitor. In so doing she took good care of the oldest and most useless of things: on one of the cupboards lay an old child's toy that hadn't been used for a long while now and perhaps never would be again—it was a little whistle, part of which was round and hollow, and in this were things that rattled; she wiped it clean all over and put it back.

"But why don't you say anything?" she said suddenly, appearing to notice the silence that reigned all around.

"Because all the enjoyment's gone out of my life," Victor replied.

At this the woman didn't say a word, not one syllable, but continued with her wiping down and her periodic shaking out of the cloth at the open window.

After a while she said, "I've put out the suitcase and boxes upstairs for you. As you were out and about yesterday, I spent the whole day at it. I've laid out your clothes

17

all together as they should be packed in the suitcase. The linen, too, which has been mended, is lying next to them. You'll have to attend to the books yourself, and also to what you're thinking of putting in the knapsack. I've bought you a suitcase of fine soft leather, the sort you once said you liked so much. But where are you going, Victor?"

"To pack."

"Good heavens, child, you haven't eaten yet. Wait a moment. It'll certainly be warm by now."

Victor waited. She went out and returned with two saucepans, a bowl, and cup and a white roll, all on a round, clean, brass-rimmed tray. She set this down, poured out the milk, tasted it to see that it was good and properly warm and then pushed the whole tray in front of the boy, leaving it to the aroma of all this to entice him or not. And in fact her experience didn't let her down, for the boy, who began to taste only a little at first, finally sat down again and ate with all the pleasure and gusto so characteristic of youth.

Meanwhile she slowly brought her work to an end and, putting away her cleaning cloths, cast the occasional glance towards him, smiling warmly. When he had eventually polished off everything she had brought him, she gave what little remained to the dog and carried the crockery back into the kitchen for it to be washed up by the maid when she got back home, for the girl had gone down to the church square in the valley to buy the various things needed for that day.

When the woman came back from the kitchen, she

sat down in front of Victor and said: "Now that you're refreshed, listen to me. If I were indeed your mother, as you always call me, I would be really cross with you, Victor, for, look, I have to tell you that what you said a moment ago about all the enjoyment having gone out of your life is very wrong of you. How wrong, you don't as yet understand. Even if it was something sad that was awaiting you, you still shouldn't say such a thing. Look at me, Victor, I'll soon be seventy years old and still haven't said that the enjoyment has gone out of my life because everything, everything should give you pleasure, for the world is so beautiful and grows even more beautiful the longer you live. But I must confess to you—and you, too, will come to have the same experience as me when you're older—that when I was eighteen years old, I, too, was always saying that I didn't enjoy life any more—I said it in fact whenever a particular pleasure I had set my heart on was denied me. At that time I would wish away all the time that separated me from a future pleasure and did not consider what a precious and good thing time was. Only when you get older do you learn properly to treasure things, and treasure time, too, which becomes shorter and shorter. Everything that God sends us is beautiful, even though we may not understand it—and we only need to give it some proper thought to see that what God gives is just sheer happiness; the suffering is what *we* add to it. Didn't you see, when you came in, how the lettuces by the fence that you could barely see any sign of yesterday, have all sprouted today?

"No," replied Victor, "I didn't."

"I looked at them before sunrise and was so pleased," said the woman. "From now on I'm going to make sure no one can ever say they saw me shed a tear in sorrow, even if I have occasion to feel it, for sorrow is after all only another kind of joy. In my youth I went through a lot of sorrow—great, burning sorrow, but it was all to my good and betterment—often leading to earthly happiness even. I am telling you all this, Victor, because you're leaving soon. You should be very grateful to God, my child, that you have young limbs and a healthy body that enable you to go out into the world and seek out all those joys and delights that don't just fall into our laps of themselves. See now, you have no inheritance—your father was himself to blame for much of the misfortune that befell him here in this world; in the next he will certainly be eternally blessed, for he was a good man and always had a gentle heart, like you. When, according to the instructions of your deceased father's will, you were brought here to live with me, to learn in the village the things you'd later be required to know in the town, you had next to nothing. But you grew up and now you've even landed the job so many others applied for and for which they envy you. The fact that you must leave now is nothing and is in the natural order of things, for all men must leave their mothers and get down to work. You've experienced lots of good things and should therefore thank God in your prayers for having given you so much and should feel humbled that you have the gifts to deserve it. In a nutshell, Victor, I would be very cross with you for what you said if I were your mother, because you don't recognise the hand of the Lord God. But because I'm not your mother, I'm not sure whether I have given you enough love and care to have the right to get angry with you and to say this: that it's not right of you, my child, nor is it at all a good thing to have said."

"But I didn't mean it the way you think, Mother," said Victor.

"I know, my child, and don't trouble yourself too much over what I've said," replied the mother. "I must now tell you as well, Victor, that you are not nearly as poor as you may think. I have often told you how astonished I was—joyfully astonished, that is—when I learnt that your father had laid down in his will that you were to be brought up here with me. He knew me very well and put his trust in me. I don't believe that trust will prove to have been misplaced. Victor, my dear, precious child, I'll tell you now what you have. Linen—the choicest of all the things we wear, since it is worn closest to our body, protecting it and keeping it healthy—of this you have so much that you can change it daily, as you have learnt to do here. We have mended everything so that there's not a damaged thread to be found. As for the future, you will never lack for anything you need. Outside Hanna is bleaching garments, half of which are earmarked for you—and the knitting, sewing and mending we'll take care of. You have a decent wardrobe in other respects, too: three different changes of clothing, not counting what you have on now. Everything is now of a finer order than you have been used to so far, for a man taking up his first post, Victor, is like a bridegroom needing to be properly fitted out—and, like a bridegroom, he also should be in a state of grace. The money they had to give me over the years for your keep I have saved and always added the interest. Now that's all yours. Your guardian doesn't know that and doesn't need to either, for after all you must have some spending money when others are around, otherwise you'll feel awkward. If your uncle takes what is left of the small estate, you shouldn't let it upset you because there are so many debts attached to it that there's barely a single roof-tile left that's not owed. I was at the records office and had them look it up for you so as to be sure. And you'll still get regular emergency funds from me, too. So everything is fine. You have to make the journey to your uncle before you take up your post because he wishes it. Who knows what good will come of it—that's all new to you yet. Your guardian also recognises the necessity for you to comply with your uncle's wish that you journey to him on foot. Did you see Rosina yesterday?"

"No, Mother, we got back late in the evening and ate in Ferdinand's room—and today I set off at daybreak because there's so much to do. My guardian said I should start my journey on foot from town and in this way take my leave of them all."

"See now, Victor, if you work hard at your profession, you might well marry Rosina one day. She is very beautiful, and think what a powerful man her father is. He has carried out the burdensome role of guardian in a just and diligent manner and is fond of you, for he was always very pleased when you did well in your exams. But enough of that—such a marriage is a long way off yet. Your father might now have been as highly placed, or higher even, for he had a strong intellect, but this was simply not recognised. Not even your own blood mother recognised it. And he was good, so very good that even now I sometimes find myself thinking what a really good man he was. Your mother, too, was a dear and pious woman, but she died when you were so young, far too young. Don't be sad, Victor—go up to your room now and sort everything out. Don't rearrange the clothes—they are already laid out so just pack them into the suitcase as they are. Be careful as you put them in that nothing gets too creased ... So ... Before you go up, Victor, listen to one more request from your foster-mother: when you see Hanna again, today or tomorrow, speak nicely to her—it isn't right that you haven't always got on well together. So, Victor, go now, for one day is not at all long."

The young man gave no answer but stood up and left the room like someone whose heart is weighed down with melancholy. And as inner emotion often makes one clumsy with outer things, so it was with him, too, so that he knocked his shoulder against the frame of the door. The dog went upstairs with him.

Up in his room, which had been his for so many years now, a bleak sight met him, for nothing was in the place it had used to occupy in the peaceful, unbroken times gone by. The one exception to this was the large elder bush onto which his window looked out, with the rippling water beneath that was reflected on the ceiling of his room in fine, trembling glimmerings of light; there, still, were the sunlit and silent hills ranged protectively around the valley, at the bottom of which lay the orchard, which, with its clustering abundance, enfolded the village and rested in the warm air caught between the hills, bringing blessing and fruitfulness. Everything else was different. The drawers of the chests had been pulled out and were empty, and their contents lay round about: the snow-white linen arranged according to type; then the clothes, neatly laid together and sorted into appropriate piles; other things, some of which were to be packed in the suitcase while others belonged in the knapsack that was already open and lay waiting on a chair. On the bed were unfamiliar objects, on the floor was the suitcase, its straps loosened, and with torn paper lying about: the pocket watch, however, hanging in its usual place, was still ticking, and the books, too, were still ranged in the bookcases, waiting to be read.

Victor looked at all this but did nothing. Instead of packing, he sat down on a chair that stood in the corner of the room and pressed the dog to his heart. And there he remained.

The chimes of the clocktower striking the hour came in through the open windows but Victor didn't know what time it was—the maid, who had returned, could be heard singing down in the garden—now and again a gleam of light flashed on the distant hills as if a bright piece of silver or glass pane were lying there—the glimmering light on the ceiling had ceased because the sun had already risen too high over the house—one could just make out the horn of the shepherd driving his flock on the mountains—the clock struck once more: but the young man remained sitting there on his chair, and in front of him the dog sat motionless, looking at him.

At last, when he heard his mother's footsteps coming up the stairs, he leapt up suddenly and threw himself into his work. He flung open the doors of the bookcase and quickly and mechanically began to take out the books and lay them on the floor. However, the woman stuck her head round the open door for a second only and, seeing him so busy, she withdrew and went away on tiptoe. Having got started, though, the boy stuck to it and continued working with a passion.

All the books were taken out of the two bookcases until they were empty and the bare shelves were staring blankly into the room. Then he tied the books together into bundles and put them into a box standing there for this purpose. When the books were thus stored away, he screwed down the lid and stuck a label on it. Then he turned to his papers. All the drawers of the writing desk and the two other tables were pulled out and all the documents in them examined one after the other. Some of these were quickly scanned only and set down in special places for immediate packing, others were read, many were torn up and thrown onto the floor, and many put into his coat pocket or wallet. Finally, when all the table drawers were also empty, with nothing in them except the sad dust that had slowly settled inside over the years and the cracks that had formed meanwhile in the wood, he then tied the piles of documents also into bundles and put them in the suitcase. Then he turned to the clothes and the packing of the suitcase. Many souvenirs of earlier times, such as a small silver candlestick, a box with a gold chain, a telescope, two small pistols and finally his beloved flute, were all stowed away among the soft, protective linen. When everything was done, the lid was closed, the straps secured, the padlock fastened and an address label stuck on top. The suitcase and the box had to be sent on ahead, while the knapsack, which was still sitting on the chair, needed to contain all the things he would be taking with him on his journey on foot. He quickly packed this until it was full and then fastened the straps.

With everything now finished, he looked around him in the room and at the walls to see if there wasn't something lying about or hanging up that remained to be packed, but there was nothing more and the room stared back at him with a ravaged look. Still standing among the jumble of unfamiliar objects and equally unfamiliar effects was the one bed, but this, too, had been soiled with dust or covered with torn pieces of paper. He stood there for a moment. The dog, who until then had watched the proceedings with deep suspicion, not allowing a single movement, whether to the right or the left, to escape its attention, and sometimes getting in the boy's way, now stood quietly in front of him looking up, as if to say: "Now what?"

Victor, however, wiped the sweat from his forehead with the flat of his hand and his handkerchief, picked up a brush lying there, brushed the dust from his clothes and went downstairs.

Here meanwhile a long time had passed and things had changed. There was no one in the sitting-room. The morning sun that had shone in through the windows in such friendly fashion when he had arrived from town early that day, making the curtains glow so brilliantly white, had now turned into a midday sun and was directly above the roof, pouring down its dazzling light and warm rays onto the grey wood. The fruit trees stood there peacefully, their leaves, which in the morning had been so wet and sparkling and which were now dry and shone but more dully—these are now motionless, and in their branches the birds are pecking at their food. The curtains have been pulled back, the windows are open and the hot countryside looks in. In the kitchen a glowing, smokeless fire is burning, and standing next to it the maid, who is cooking. Everything is in that state of deep peace of which the pagans once said: "Pan is sleeping."

Victor went into the kitchen and asked where his mother was.

"In the garden, or somewhere around," the maid replied.

And where is Hanna?" Victor enquired further.

"She was here a moment ago," answered the maid. "I don't know where she went."

Victor went out into the garden and walked down between neat flower beds he had known so long, and where everything was budding and sprouting. The gardener was setting out plants and his little son was pumping water, as he had often seen them do. Victor asked about his mother: they hadn't seen her in the garden. He carried on walking past blackcurrants, goose-berries, fruit-trees and hedges. Tall grass grew between the trunks and in the borders many flowers were blooming. From the area of the greenhouse, whose windows in this heat were standing open, a voice rang out: "Victor, Victor!"

The one thus called, whose misery at his impending departure had partly lifted as a result of his feverish work in his room upstairs, brightened and turned his face towards the greenhouses. There a beautiful, slim girl was standing waving at him. Leaving the path, he walked straight across to her through the grass.

"There you are already, Victor," she said, when he had reached her. "I had no idea—when did you come?"

"Very early this morning, Hanna!"

"I went shopping with the maid, that's why I didn't see you arrive. And where have you been since?"

"I've been packing up my things in my room."

"Mother said nothing about your being here already so I thought you would perhaps have slept in a bit and not set off from town until the afternoon."

"That was a foolish thought, Hanna. Am I one to sleep all morning? Or a weakling who needs to rest up after a walk the day before? Or do you think it's a great distance, perhaps, or that I'd choose the heat of midday to walk in?"

"Why didn't you look across to our house, Victor, as you were all passing by yesterday?"

"Because we were celebrating Ferdinand's birthday and with the agreement of the parents the whole day belonged to us. And so no father, mother or anyone else was allowed to give us orders. That's why our village was simply the place where we wanted to eat lunch, because it's so beautiful, and for no other reason. Don't you understand that?"

"No. Because I would have looked across."

"That's because you get everything mixed up, because you're inquisitive and can't control yourself. Now where is Mother? I've got something important to tell her—it just wasn't immediately clear to me when she was talking to me, but now I know what I should say in reply."

"She's doing the bleaching."

"Then that's where I must go."

"Then go, Victor," said the girl, turning round the corner of the greenhouse.

Immediately and without paying her special attention, Victor went towards the place he knew well, where the bleaching was done.

This was a place behind the garden with short, velvety grass on which the linen lay spread out everywhere in long strips. There the mother was standing looking at the bountiful snowy folds at her feet. Every so often she would try certain places to see whether they were dry yet, every so often fasten a loop to the peg with which the linen was stretched out on the ground, and every so often hold the flat of her hand above her eyes like a little roof and look round about her.

Victor went up to her.

"Have you finished already," she said, "or have you left some of it for the afternoon? It's a lot, isn't it, however little it appears. You've walked a long way today—do the rest after lunch, or tomorrow. I could have packed it all myself yesterday—I wanted to—but I thought to myself he must do it himself so he learns how."

"No, Mother," he replied, "there's nothing left to do—it's all done."

"Really?" the mother said. "Here, let me see."

So saying, she reached out towards his forehead and he bent towards her a little. She brushed back a lock of hair that had flopped over his face while he had been working, and said: "You're really flushed."

"It's the warm weather," he replied.

"No, no, it's the work you've been doing, too. And if it *is* all done, then you'll have to stay in your travelling clothes today and tomorrow, too, and what will you do then all that time?"

"I'll walk up to the brook, to the beech wood and round that way. I'll keep these clothes on. But I came out here for something else, Mother, and would like to say something but it will make you cross."

"Don't scare me like that, child—let's hear it. Is there something you want still? Is there something missing?"

"No, nothing's missing—rather there's too much of something. You spoke of something today, Mother, which didn't sink in immediately at the time but which I now can't get out of my mind."

"What was that then, Victor?"

"You said you were assigned a sum of money for my keep and this you were to receive every year. You said that you received this money—and you said furthermore that you invested the money and also regularly added to it the interest that accrued."

"Yes, that's what I said and what I did."

"Look, Mother, my conscience tells me it's not right for me to accept money from you because it doesn't belong to me—and so I have come to tell you this nicely in advance, rather than decline the money later and anger you. Are you cross?"

"No, I'm not cross," she said beaming at him, her eyes lit up with joy, "but don't be a foolish child, Victor! You must see that I didn't take you into my house for gain—I would never have taken a child in for gain—that's why what was left over every year from the money is rightly yours. Listen to me and I'll explain. Your guardian provided for your clothing; as regards food, you didn't involve me in any expense—like a bird you scarcely ate anything, and the vegetables and fruit and other things you enjoyed, we had all that here. Do you see now? And the fact that I grew so fond of you wasn't something with which your father charged me and wasn't written down in any will either, so you can't do anything about that. Do you understand everything now?"

"No, I don't, and it's not what you say, either. Once again your kindness is so great that you make me feel nothing but shame. If something really were left over every year after costs had been deducted and you had held this in trust for me, then that would indeed have been just a loving and kind act, but now you say that everything is left over—something almost painful to hear. You have besides done what can scarcely be explained:

not only did you give me a lovely room but you also put in it the very things I loved and which meant a lot to me; you provided me with food and drink and yourself with nothing but work. What's more you have now bought everything for my journey; you have scrimped and saved from the field and garden produce so as to fill my case with beautiful linen and other things—and when in former times I had everything I needed, so you would go about giving me something more—and, on top of that, every day you would secretly leave something out for me that you thought I would love. You have loved me more than Hanna!"

"No, Victor dear, that's not right, what you say of me. You don't yet understand how feelings work. Only what comes from the heart reaches into other hearts. Hanna is my dear daughter—she is the fruit of my body and the beating of my heart ushered her into this world when I gave birth to her: this happiness was my lot late in life at a time when I might have been her grandmother—it was in the midst of the grief at her father's death that I gave birth to her, but joyfully—then I brought her up—and that made her more precious to me. But I have loved you, too, Victor, very much. Since the time you came to this house and while you were growing up I have loved you very much. Often I felt as if I really had in fact given birth to you myself—and I should in fact have been the one to give birth to you; it was the will of God, even though it turned out differently afterwards—I'll tell you about that when you're older. Finally—and to honour both God and the truth I tell you this—you have both become equally dear to me. As regards the money, let's do it like this, Victor: one should never force anyone to act against their conscience so I won't try and persuade you any longer—let's leave the matter of the money where it stands; I'll have it put in writing that it is to be given to you and Hanna when you are of age; then you can divide it between yourselves or dispose of it in any way you both see fit. Is that all right by you, Victor?"

"Yes, then I can give it all to her."

"Let's leave it at that for the moment. When the time comes, it will, I am sure, become clear what should happen to the money. I want to say one more thing in response to the other thing you said, Victor. Whenever I secretly did something good for you, I did the same for Hanna, too. Mothers are like that. From the time you came to us here it is almost as if we had been blessed even more. I was able to save every year for Hanna more than before. Caring for two is easier, you get more practised at it, and where God has blessings for two, he often gives for three … Oh, Victor, how quickly the time has gone by since you came here. When I think back to when I was once young, then I have to ask—Where have the years gone and how did I become so old? For everything is still as beautiful as yesterday—the mountains are still there, the sun is shining down on them and the years have gone by as if in the space of a day. When you walk up into the woods once again this afternoon, like you said, or tomorrow perhaps, then look for a spot—you might almost be able to see it from here—do you see, up there in the gully where the light seems to be rippling down over the green

33

beech trees? The spot is important for you. A spring rises there and then flows down into the gully; above the spring there is a broad flat stone and next to it a very old beech tree with a long, low-hanging branch on which you can spread out clothes or hang a woman's hat."

"I don't know the spot, Mother, but if you wish I'll walk up there and find it."

"No, Victor, it doesn't in fact mean as much to you as it does to me—you'll also know other spots which to your eyes may be more beautiful. Let's leave that now. Everything will be fine—don't think about the money any more and don't be sad. You're feeling the pain of separation already, I know, and that's why you're taking things more to heart than they warrant. You said you wanted to walk up to the beech wood before today is out: haven't you noticed though that not a single little branch is stirring in the garden and how the tops of the trees seem to be frozen in the air; I think a storm might be on the way—you shouldn't go too far."

"I won't go too far—and I know well the signs of a storm; if I see any, I'll come back home."

"Yes, Victor, do that and it'll be good. Would you like to go inside into the sitting-room with me in a minute— it's nearly midday already—or would you prefer to stay out here until lunchtime?"

"I'd like to stay in the garden for a little while."

"Stay in the garden then. I'll just fasten the loops here and check that the hens haven't dirtied the linen again."

He remained with her a while longer, looking on. Then he went into the garden and she watched him go, after which she fastened first one loop, then the next, until they were all secure. She wiped away a small piece of earth that the foot of a goose or something else had carried onto the linen. She then lifted first this and then another spot to air it, so the linen wouldn't cling to the grass too much. And every time she looked up she would turn in the direction Victor had gone and watch him standing in front of one or another bush or walking about or looking out over the fence into the surrounding area. This lasted until suddenly the midday chimes rang out in the still, warm air—the signal for prayers for the community and for this house, according to long custom, the signal also that they should come together for the midday meal. Victor's mother saw him turn round as the clock rang out and head for the house. She then followed him.

When the young man entered the house, he saw that guests had arrived in the meantime, namely his guardian and his family. As often happens in such matters, they had wanted to give Victor a surprise and at the same time spend a day in the country.

"You can see, my dear ward," the guardian said to the astonished young man, "what nice people we are. We wanted to see you again today and give you a good sending-off party. This way you can take a straight course over the hills the day after tomorrow, or whenever your travel preparations are finished, without first coming into town to take your leave of us, as we had arranged. Be sure now that you enjoy your last few days of freedom before you have to take on the yoke of hard work."

"Greetings, dear boy," said the guardian's wife and kissed Victor on his forehead just as he was about to bend down to kiss her hand.

"Good the way it's turned out, eh?" said Ferdinand, their son, shaking his friend's hand.

Rosina, the daughter, a truly beautiful twelve-year-old girl, was standing to one side looking around happily and saying nothing.

Victor's foster-mother must have known about the planned visit, for the table was laid for precisely the number of people who were there. She greeted everyone very warmly as she came in, organised who was to sit where and said: "Do you see how fond everyone is of you, Victor?"

The food arrived and the meal began.

Victor's guardian and his wife sat at the head of the table, his foster-sister, Hanna, was put beside Rosina, the boys opposite the girls, and his mother, as hostess, had put herself at the bottom, since she would be coming and going a lot while seeing to her guests.

The country fare was much enjoyed.

Victor's guardian told of adventures he had had when travelling as a student, laid down rules concerning a measured enjoyment of what pleasures the world offered, and advised Victor as to how he should behave in the immediate future. His wife alluded to a future bride, and Ferdinand promised he would visit his friend as soon as the latter had taken up his post. Victor spoke little and promised to abide closely by everything his guardian recommended and had impressed upon him.

He also promised to take good care of the letter his guardian had given him to take to his uncle, and to surrender it to him immediately on his arrival. It was to the house of this uncle that Victor was now to travel, and, as his uncle had expressly insisted, on foot, a strange and somewhat capricious condition.

Towards evening the townsfolk set off back home. They got their carriage, which had stopped at the inn, to go on ahead of them along the narrower valley to the point where it opened out into the wider one, and thus far their hostess and Victor and Hanna accompanied them.

"Goodbye, Frau Ludmilla," said Victor's guardian, as he got into the carriage. "Goodbye, Victor, and remember to do everything I told you."

When he had climbed into the carriage and when Victor had thanked him again and they had all taken their leave of each other, the horses sprang into action and set off.

By now it was too late for Victor to go for a long walk up into the woods so he remained at home, looked at a number things in the garden, and inspected once more all his belongings packed in his knapsack.

III

PARTING

THE NEXT DAY, the last Victor was to spend in this house, brought with it nothing out of the ordinary. There was much packing still; things already organised were reorganised; as is very common in such cases, everyone acted as if nothing were to happen—and so the morning was soon over.

After lunch, when they had barely got down from the table, Victor at once went off alone up to the stream for a walk, heading for the beech wood and its stone slopes.

"Let him go, let him go," the old woman told herself. "He'll be feeling heavy-hearted."

"Where is Victor, Mother?" Hanna asked at one point during the course of the afternoon.

"He has gone to say goodbye," she answered, "gone to say goodbye to his old haunts. Dear God, he has nothing else, after all. His guardian, as excellent and as prudent a man as he is, is not close to him—nor are his guardian's family."

Hanna said nothing in reply to these words—not the slightest sound did she make by way of reply, but walked off, disappearing between the spreading branches of the little plum-trees.

The rest of the afternoon passed as usual: the people spent the time with whatever work came their way, the birds twittered the time away in their trees, the hens strutted around in the yard, the grass and the plants grew a little taller and the mountains decked themselves in the gold of evening.

When the sun had disappeared from the sky and only the pale gold crest of the hill loomed ominously over the valley—ominously because tomorrow morning early it would again be looming pale gold above the valley, beckoning away forever someone who was so loved—when this hillcrest was glimmering above the valley, Victor came back from the walk he had set off on so hurriedly after lunch. He walked along the garden fence in order to reach the little gate that led into the house from the linen-bleaching area. The white strips of linen were no longer there, only the greener and damper grass showed where they had been lying during the day—there were many glass frames covering the beds since the clear sky promised a cool night—a thin column of smoke rose from the house because his mother was perhaps getting supper ready. Victor had turned his face towards the evening sky, which it softly illumined, while the cooler air ruffled his hair and the sky was reflected in his doleful eyes.

Hanna had seen him pass quite close by her, since she'd been standing just inside the garden fence, but she hadn't had the courage to address him. The girl was busy picking pieces of silk material off a roughly trimmed bush; these pieces were part of a separate dress and had been dyed and placed on the bush to dry during the day. She was now taking them off one by one and laying them together in a small heap. When she looked round after a while, she saw Victor standing in the garden next to the large rose-hedge.

Later she saw him again standing by the blue lilac hedge, which was already in bud. The lilac, however, was much nearer to her than the rose-hedge. Then he moved on again and finally came over to her and said: "I'd like to help you carry something in, Hanna."

"No, it's all right thank you, Victor," she replied, "they're just some small pieces of material that I dyed and left here to dry."

"Hasn't the sun rather taken the colour out?"

"No. You have to lay this blue out in the sun, best of all in the spring sun—then it'll be even more beautiful."

"And is it?"

"Look!"

"Oh, I don't understand any of that."

"Not as beautiful as the ribbons last year but certainly beautiful enough."

"It's a very fine silk."

"Very fine."

"Is there an even finer one?"

"Yes, there are ones even finer, much finer."

"And would you like to have lots of beautiful silk clothes?"

"No. They're really excellent as garments for special occasions but since you don't need many of these, I wouldn't want much silk. Other clothes are beautiful, too, and wearing silk is always a proud business."

"Isn't the silkworm a wretched little thing?"

"Why, Victor?"

"Because it has to be killed if you want to get its silk web."

"Does it?"

"Yes, you boil its web in water vapour or smoke it in sulphur so that the creature inside dies, for otherwise it would eat its way through the threads and emerge as a butterfly."

"Poor creature!"

"Yes—and nowadays we take it away from its poor native land too, Hanna, where it was able to crawl about on sunny mulberry trees, and we feed it in our living rooms on leaves that grow outdoors and aren't as luxuriant either as they are in their country of origin. And swallows, storks and other migratory birds leave us in the autumn for foreign lands far, far away perhaps, but they return in the spring. The world really must be huge, really huge."

"My poor Victor, don't talk about such things."

"I'd like to ask you about something, Hanna."

"Then ask me, Victor."

"I want to thank you again very much for making me that lovely purse, Hanna. The fabric is so fine and the colours are really beautiful. I've kept it safe and won't put any money in it."

"Oh, Victor, that was a long time ago that I gave you that purse and you shouldn't go to the trouble of thanking me. Go ahead and put your money in it—I'll make you a new one when it wears out, then another and so on, so that you never lack for anything. I've made you something else for your journey that is far more beautiful than the purse but Mother didn't want me to give it to you until this evening or tomorrow morning."

"That makes me really happy, Hanna."

"Where were you all afternoon, Victor?"

"I went up to the stream as I felt so bored. I watched the water bustling so hurriedly on its way down to our village, watched how dark it gets and then so clear again, how it tries to dodge the stones and the sand only to end up in the village, but it doesn't stop there. I looked at the rock overhang that stands there gazing forever into the rippling water. Finally I went up to the beech-wood where, in one, two or even ten years' time, the tree trunks will be beautiful. Mother told me about a place where a flat stone lies across a brook and where an old beech tree stands with a long, low-lying branch. I couldn't find the spot."

"That's the beech brook at Hirschkar. There are good blackberries growing around there—I know the place well and can show you where it is tomorrow if you like."

"I won't be here any more tomorrow, Hanna."

"Oh that's right, you won't be here any more tomorrow. I keep on thinking you'll always be here."

"Oh, no. Dear Hanna, do divide up these silk strips—I really want to help you take them inside."

"I don't understand the way you are today, Victor; these things are so light a child would be able to carry ten times the amount."

"It's not because of the weight, I just want to carry them for you."

"Well, carry some, then—I'll put them together now. If you want to go in, we'll quickly gather up what remains and go."

"No, no, I don't want to go in—it isn't that late—I want to stay a bit longer in the garden. And it wasn't just about the purse that I wanted to talk to you."

"What, then, Victor? Tell me."

"The four doves I've been looking after—I know they're not that beautiful but I feel really sorry for them if no one's going to look after them now."

"I'll take care of that, Victor—I'll open the dovecot for them in the morning and close it in the evening; I'll spread sand for them and feed them."

"Then I must also thank you for all the linen I'm taking with me."

"For goodness' sake, I didn't give it to you—Mother did. Also we've still got enough in our cupboards not to feel its loss."

"The little silver box that belonged to my dead mother—you know, the one you've always liked that looks like a miniature chest with the broken filigree and the little key—I didn't pack it because I'm leaving it behind for you as a present."

"No, it's too beautiful, I can't take that."

"Please take it, Hanna—you'll be doing me a very great favour if you take it."

"If I'm doing you a great favour, then I'll take it and keep it for you until you come, and look after it carefully for you."

"And the carnations by the fence, tend them too, the poor things, do you hear—and don't forget the dog; he's old, it's true, but he's a loyal creature."

"No, Victor, I won't forget him."

"But that's not everything I actually want to say—there's something else I must say."

"Let's hear it, then, Victor!"

"Mother said I should speak nicely to you today because more often we've squabbled with each other—I want to say something good before I leave for ever—and so I came to ask you, Hanna, not to be angry with me."

"What on earth are you saying—at no time in my whole life have I been angry with you."

"Oh, I know that now too well—you've always patiently put up with my cruelty."

"Victor, don't frighten me—you've only felt this way today."

"No, you've always been good—I just didn't realise it. Listen, Hanna, I want to pour out all my heart to you: I can't describe to you how unhappy I am."

"Dear God! Victor, my dear Victor, what is it that's troubling you?"

"All day I've been choking with tears that I've had to hold back from falling. When I walked up after lunch to the sad little brook and the beech walk, it wasn't that I was bored but rather so that no eyes might see me—and I thought, I have no one in the whole wide world, no father, no mother, no sister. My uncle is threatening to take the little I do have because my father was in debt to him, and I have to leave the only people who have been good to me."

"Oh, Victor, dear Victor, don't grieve too much. Your father and your mother are dead, it's true, but that was a long time ago, so you barely knew them. Instead you found another mother who loves you as if she really were yours—and in all this time you have never had to suffer grief at the loss of your dead parents. The fact that we must now part is very, very sad; but don't wrong God, Victor, for putting us to the test. Bear it without complaint—I've borne it, too, all day long and haven't complained; and I would have continued to, as well, even if you had never come and said another word to me."

"Oh, Hanna, Hanna!"

"And even when you're no longer here we'll be thinking about what to send you, we'll be praying for you and I'll go into the garden every day and look at the hills you walked over when you left."

"No, don't do that—otherwise it would be altogether too wretched."

"Why?"

"Because it's all no use—and because it's not just the fact that I have to leave and that we have to part."

"But what, then?"

"It's because everything's all over and because I'm the loneliest creature on God's earth."

"But Victor, Victor."

"I'll never marry—impossible—it'll never be possible. So you see I won't have a home, won't belong to anyone; others will forget me—and that's good. Do you understand? —I never realised but now it's so clear—so clear. Can't you see?—But why are you suddenly so silent, Hanna?"

"Victor!"

"What, Hanna?"

"Did you think this before?"

"I did."

"And now?"

"Now—now—it's all in vain, all futile."

"Be faithful to her, Victor!"

"For ever, for ever—but it's futile."

"But why?"

"Didn't I tell you? My uncle is taking from me the only property remaining. She is well off; I am poor and won't be able to support a wife for a long, long time yet. So some suitor will come along who will support her, who will be able to give her beautiful clothes and gifts, and she will accept him."

"No, no, no, Victor, she won't—she'll never do that. She will love you all her life, as you do her, and will never leave you, as you won't leave her."

"Oh, dear, dear Hanna!"

"Dear Victor!"

"And a time will surely come when I'll come back again—and then I'll never be impatient and we'll live like brother and sister who love each other above everything, everything that this world could ever offer, and who will remain true to each other for ever and ever."

"For ever and ever," she said, quickly taking hold of his outstretched hands.

They burst into tears, weeping bitterly.

Victor drew her gently to him and she complied. She leant her head and face against his coat and, as if all the floodgates had now, so to speak, been opened, she wept and sobbed so hard, as if her heart were breaking because she was having to lose him. He put a protective and comforting arm around her and pressed her to his heart. He held her to him more and more tightly like some helpless creature. She nestled against him as against a brother who is now so very, very dear. He stroked her hair, which she wore parted, and which he then bent down and kissed—but she lifted her face up to his and kissed him passionately on his lips, more passionately than she ever thought she could kiss anything.

They then stood for a while without speaking.

Then the gardener's boy came and told them their mother had sent him to let them know they could come to supper.

They were still holding the silk strips that had begun their conversation but these were crumpled and many were wet with Hanna's tears. They therefore put these together as best they could and went hand-in-hand up the garden path towards the house. When the mother saw them coming and noticed her children's tear-reddened eyes, she smiled and had them go into the dining-room.

The meal was brought in and the mother served both of them with what she believed they liked best; she didn't ask what they had been talking about, and so all three of them ate together just as they had always eaten together every evening before now.

Hanna had very large brown eyes that were constantly and for no reason filling with tears during the meal.

When they had finished and before they got ready for bed, Hanna's present had to be fetched. It was a wallet lined with snow-white silk and contained the travel money that the mother had put inside it.

"I'll take the money out," said Victor, " and keep the wallet."

"No, no," said the mother, "leave the money where it is; see how lovely the crisp, printed notes look lying against the white silk. Among other things Hanna will always have to keep you supplied with wallets."

"I'll take very good care of it," Victor replied.

His mother then locked the side of the wallet containing the money with the tiny little key, which she showed him how to hide.

This done she shooed them off to bed.

"Never mind that," she said, when she saw that Victor was about to thank her for the travel money, "off to bed with you both. You, Victor, have to be up in the hills by five o'clock tomorrow morning. I've seen to it that the farm-hand wakes us in time, in case I should oversleep. Before you set off you must get a good solid breakfast down you. So, children, good night and sleep well."

While saying this, she had lit two candles for the children, as she did every evening; they both took their own from the table, respectfully wished their mother a good night and went to their rooms.

Victor was not yet ready for his bed. The multitude of bulky shadows thrown by the things stacked around made the room inhospitable. He went to one of the windows and looked out. The elder bush had become a black clump and the water was no longer visible: where it should have been flowing, in its place was a dark slab—only the occasional glint of light showed that it was there and moving; when all the voices of the house and village had fallen silent, a soft, soft trickling sound could also be heard coming in through the open window from this friend, which had over so many years flowed past the boy's sleeping quarters. Thousands of stars were burning in the night-sky but not a single glimmer of light from the moon, not even the thinnest sickle.

Victor finally lay down on his bed to sleep his last night here where he had spent his life for as long as he had been able to think, and to await the morning which was to take him away perhaps for ever.

That morning came very quickly. Hardly had Victor, so he thought, begun take those first deep, refreshing breaths of sleep when he heard a soft knocking on his door and the voice of his mother, who had needed no farmhand to wake her: "It's four o'clock, Victor. Get dressed, don't forget anything and then come downstairs, do you hear me?"

"I hear you, mother."

She went back downstairs but he jumped out of bed. In the double grip of the pain of leaving and the thrill of travel, he got dressed and went downstairs to the dining-room. In the dim morning light he could see breakfast already laid out on the table—never had they eaten so early. They ate in silence. Victor's foster-mother looked at Victor almost unflinchingly; Hanna didn't trust herself to raise her eyes and look at anything. Victor soon stopped eating. He rose from his chair and gathered himself. After walking round the room a couple of times, he then said: "It's time, Mother—I'll leave now."

He put the knapsack over his shoulders, tightening the

straps so it was firmly positioned. Then he picked up his hat, put his hand to his chest to see if he had his wallet and checked to see if there was anything at all he had forgotten. After this he stepped forward towards his mother, who with Hanna had got to her feet, and said: "Thank you, dear Mother, for everything … "

He could scarcely bring himself to say anything more and she anyway didn't let him continue. She led him to the consecrated water by the door, sprinkled him with a few drops, made the sign of the cross on his forehead, mouth and chest, and said: "So, my child, be off with you now. Stay as good as you've always been till now and be sure your heart remains kind and loving. Write often and be sure to say if there's anything you need. God will surely bless the road you tread, since you have always followed Him."

At these words the tears began to trickle down her face, her lips continued only to move and she was unable to say anything.

After a moment she braced herself again and said: "You'll find the boxes and the suitcase upstairs waiting for you at your destination when you arrive. Take good care of the money and the letters of recommendation your guardian gave you, don't get overheated and don't drink anything chilled. All will be well. Going away is not such a bad thing and everywhere you will find good people, who will be well-disposed towards you. If I hadn't lived so long in our hills and by the apple-tree, then I would love to travel to strange parts. And so farewell, my Victor, farewell."

With these words she kissed him on the cheeks. Silently he reached out a hand to Hanna, who was overwhelmed with weeping, and left. Outside in front of the door were also standing the servants and the gardener. Without saying anything he shook hands with all of them—they stepped to one side and he headed down the narrow garden path towards the little gate.

"How handsome he is," said his mother, almost bursting out loud into tears, as with Hanna she watched him go, "how handsome with his brown hair, his fine gait—oh, the preciousness, the vulnerability of youth, dear God!"

And the tears ran down her wet hands, which she was holding up in front of her face and eyes.

"You once told me and Victor," said Hanna, "that no one would ever see you crying again in sorrow—and now you are, Mother."

"No, my child," replied the mother, "these are tears of joy that he has grown into the young man he is. It is really strange: he never knew his father and yet, when he walked out just now, he had his father's head, his gait and bearing. He will turn out fine and my tears, my child, are tears of joy."

"Oh, not mine, not mine," said Hanna, lifting her handkerchief again to her ceaselessly streaming eyes.

Victor, meanwhile, had gone out through the gate. He passed the elder bush, crossed the two footbridges, walked past the fruit trees he had known over so many years and climbed up towards the meadows and fields. At this high point he stopped for a moment and, on hearing above the faint and indistinct sounds of the village the furious howling of the Pomeranian dog, which they had had to catch and tie up to prevent it from following him, the tears suddenly came pouring out and he almost shouted out loud: "Where will I ever find such a mother again and such creatures that so love me? The day before yesterday I was in such a great hurry to leave the town in order to spend another few hours in the valley and today I'm leaving to go somewhere else for ever and ever."

As he had finally reached a place which was no longer so far away from the highest ridge of the hill, he looked back once more for the last time. He could still make out the house, along with the garden and fence. Against the green he could see something that was as red as Hanna's shawl. But it was only a little chimney cowl.

He then walked up as far as the ridge of the hill—he did look round again—over the entire valley a radiantly beautiful day lay spread out. Then it took only a few steps for him to walk round the summit and everything had disappeared behind him, and a new valley and new horizon lay before his eyes. In the meantime the sun had risen quite high, drying the grass and his tears, sending down its warm rays to the lands beneath. He walked on, taking a steep course along the slope of the hill; on pulling out his pocket watch later, he saw that it was half-past seven.

"Now the bed will have been stripped and be looking bare," he thought, "the last object remaining to me. The linen bedclothes will have been taken out and the cold wood exposed. Or perhaps the maids are already in my room, busy making it look completely different."

And then he walked on further.

He found himself climbing higher and higher; the space between him and the house that he had left behind him grew, as did the time between his present thoughts and the last words he had spoken in the house. His path led him always across hillsides he had never crossed before—now uphill, now downhill, but always higher overall. He was glad he hadn't had to go into the town again to take his leave, since he wouldn't have wanted to have seen any of his friends today. The tenant farms and dwellings he came across lay now to his right, now to his left—every so often he met someone walking along who paid him no attention.

Midday approached and he continued walking, on and on.

The world grew bigger, grew brighter and spread wider all about him as he headed forward—and everywhere he went thousands upon thousands of creatures rejoiced.

IV

THE JOURNEY

A ND THE WORLD BECAME even bigger and brighter, with its countless beings rejoicing all around, and Victor strode from one hill to the next, one valley to the next, in his heart the heavy ache of a child and in his head fresh and wondering eyes. Every day he spent far from his home made him stronger and more capable. The barren breeze swept through his brown hair; the white clouds piled up like dazzling snow here as they did, too, in the valley of his birth; his fine cheeks had already taken on a darker hue, while on his back he carried his rucksack, in his hand a staff. The sole creature that bound him to his home was the old Pomeranian, which was running alongside him looking desperately thin. Incredibly, it was on the third day after his departure that the dog had unexpectedly caught up with him. Victor had been walking up through a wood along a cool, broad and damp path when, looking round, as he often did in order to drink in the sight of the wet pine trees glinting in the sun, he became aware of something racing towards him. But how astonished he was when, once the dark little shape had reached him, it sprang up and proved to be none other than his foster-mother's old and trusty Pomeranian. But what sort of condition the animal was in: mud had caked its beautiful fur, which was filled to the roots with white dust from the road, and its eyes were red and inflamed; when it tried to pant out whining sounds of joy, it couldn't, for its voice had become hoarse and when it tried to jump up, also for joy, it fell back on its hind legs into the ditch.

"Poor old Pom," said Victor, squatting down next to him, "do you see now what a crazy thing that was you just attempted, you silly old chap?"

But at these words the dog wagged its tail as if it had been praised to the skies.

The first thing the young man did was to wipe him down a little with a cloth so that he at least looked better. Then he took out two chunks of bread he had put into his pocket that morning in case he should run into a beggar, sat himself down on a large stone and began to break off pieces that he threw to the dog; the animal bolted them down ravenously and then carried on eyeing the boy's hands long after these were empty.

"I haven't got any more now," said Victor, "but at the first farmhouse we come to we'll buy a bowl of milk and you can have it all to yourself."

The dog seemed reassured, as if he had understood these words.

A few steps further on where a thin thread of water was running down from a moss-covered rock, Victor caught up enough water in the leather beaker his mother had given him until it was full and offered it to the dog to drink. But the latter tasted it just a little and then looked up expectantly at the boy, for he wasn't thirsty and must have drunk out of all the hundreds of ditches and streams he had passed through.

They then walked on together and at the first inn Victor wrote a letter to his mother telling her that the dog was with him and that she shouldn't worry about it.

As regards the milk, Victor was true to his word. What's more, from now on the dog was given as much to eat as it could get down; however, although in this way it managed to consume more in one day than it could barely do in three at home, the effects of the unaccustomed exertion, how dreadful God alone knew, were so great that it trotted along next to the boy, hanging, as it were, inside its own skin.

"He'll recover, I'm sure—he'll recover," the latter thought to himself, and they walked on.

Victor brooded long and hard over why the animal had on this occasion come after him, when before, on a simple command, it had stayed at home and waited for him, even when he had been away for days on end. But he then concluded rightly that the dog, whose whole life's object was to study every move its higher-ranking friend, the boy, made, had known only too well that he was leaving for ever and had therefore taken the extreme step of following him.

And so they journeyed on together now, from one hill to the next, from one meadow to the next—and often the boy might have been seen washing the dog in a meadow stream and drying its coat with grass and foliage; often, too, both might have been seen either walking quietly along next to each other, or at times when the boy stopped on some high ground and looked far and wide over the meadows, over the long strips of field, over the dark patches of copse and over at the white church-towers of the villages, while the dog stood at his master's side, looking up at him.

Often waves of corn, which must have belonged to someone, lapped against the path taken by the wayfarers, cornfields bounded by hedges that someone must have planted, while birds flew in this or that direction as if heading for their various homes. For days Victor had not spoken to a soul, apart from when greeted by some wagoner or traveller or when the inn-keeper waved his cap on his departure and said: "Have a good journey—goodbye!"

On the eighth day after he had left his foster-mother and his valley, he entered a region, which, unlike much of the inhospitable area he had walked through up to now, lay neatly and benignly alongside gentle hills, showing once again the succession of orchards characteristic of his home valley; it was an area graced with well-to-do houses and where there was not the tiniest patch of ground that was not put to use and on which there wasn't something growing. In the green countryside beyond was the silver glint of a river and further off the oh, so gentle, almost achingly enticing blue of the mountains. For some time now he had had these mountains spreading out to his left, but now they swung in a curve nearer towards his road, with the pale-coloured lights and fissures in their walls visible.

"How far is it to Attmaning?" he asked a man, sitting in the arbour of a village inn, sipping a cool drink.

"If you carry on today for a good distance, then you should be able to get there in good time tomorrow," the man replied, "but you'd have to take the footpath and then head for the mountains along the river Afel."

"I want to go Hul, actually."

"To Hul? You won't get a warm reception there. But if you're prepared to climb over the Grisel, to the right of the lake, you'll come to a jolly blacksmith I can recommend, where you'll meet a very different fate."

"I've got to go to Hul, though."

"From Attmaning it's three hours at the most."

Victor had sat down during this conversation and taken some refreshment, both for himself and the dog. After he had talked further with his neighbour about this and that, he stood up again and, following the advice of his new benefactor, travelled on a good stretch that selfsame day until he came to the Afel, a clear blue, flowing stream. At barely first light the next day he could already be seen heading towards the mountains along the footpath forking off the road that the man had recommended and which he had enquired about more closely. The massive and lofty stone bulks edged ever closer to him and in the course of the morning looked like so many welcoming and colourful paintings. He met with the noise of rushing waters, with farmers on loaded wagons; sometimes the odd man on foot, sporting a pointed hat and goatee beard—and before it struck eleven, Victor was already sitting under the roof of the inn at Attmaning, having joined the road again, and was looking out towards the mountain pass, in which everything was glimmering with blue light and where a narrow strip of water was flashing like the glint of a scythe.

Attmaning is the last place in the hill region and butts up against the high mountain chain. The bright green of its trees, the nearby mountains, its pointed church spire and sunny position make it the loveliest place that there could ever be on this earth of ours.

Victor remained sitting at his little table outside on the street—something he always greatly enjoyed—until nearly four o'clock, drinking in the sight of those great mountains, their beautiful blue colour and hazy, ever-changing lights. He had never in his life seen their like. What was the highest and most imposing hill at home in comparison to these? When it struck four and the blue shadows inched slowly down the length of the entire rock-faces, with their distance from him, which he had earlier been able to roughly judge, becoming strangely blurred, he finally enquired in which direction Hul lay.

"Up there by the lake," said the innkeeper, pointing to the mountain pass towards which Victor had looked so often during the afternoon.

"Do you want to get to Hul today, then?" he asked after a while, pointing to the pass Victor had gazed at so often in the course of the afternoon.

"Yes," said Victor, "and I want to make use of the cool of this evening to get there."

"Then you'd best not hang about," replied the the innkeeper, "and if you don't have anyone else, I'll give you my lad—he can take you up through the wood and then point out your way from there."

Victor thought in fact there was no need for a guide, for the opening between the mountains lay over there, welcoming and near, but he went along with this nevertheless and meanwhile sorted out his travel things, which he had set down.

He found it strange, though, how people speaking about Hul always said 'up there' when to his eyes the mountains there merged together with such hazy beauty that he judged the glittering lake water to be lying deep down below these, although, on the other hand, he could also see it was just from this region that the Afel came plunging and frothing down towards Attmaning.

"Here, Rudi—take the gentleman here up to the col and show him the way down into Hul," the innkeeper called into the house.

"Yes," a child's voice sounded from within.

And indeed straight away a blond-haired, red-cheeked lad appeared, and, taking in Victor with his large and friendly blue eyes, said: "So, let's go, sir."

Victor had settled his bill and was ready to set out. The boy left the inn road immediately and led him off along a stone path between densely-growing and enormous oak and sycamore trees. Soon the path began to climb and sometimes Victor could look out through the tops of the trees below onto the huge mountains, which drew ever more solemnly together and grew darker, too, the lower the sun declined. They also took on a more beautiful blue, the brighter and more shimmering the evening light painted the greenery of the trees onto their sides. Finally the woods became very dense, the deciduous trees fell away and the two travellers came into a rough area of evergreen trees, whose impenetrability was relieved only occasionally by petrified streams of cascading stone. Victor hadn't been able to see the woods from Attmaning and would never have believed such a wilderness could have lain between him and the beautiful glint of water that had beckoned behind it, from so near, it had seemed. On and on they walked. All the time Victor was thinking that now they would start the descent but the path wound continually along a slope that grew in size, making it seem as if the woods were stretching out and pushing the lake further away in front of them. The boy walked bare-foot next to him on the sharp stone scree. Finally, when nearly two hours had elapsed, the little guide stopped and said: "This is the col. If you now go down that way there—not the other one—that is, past the picture of the martyred Gilbert, and round the edge of the lake where there are lots of stones that have fallen down, you'll see some houses—that's Hul. Just keep looking through the branches to be sure you can see the water because there's also a path that leads to the Afel and a clearing—that would take you in the wrong direction."

So said the lad and, after receiving his reward from Victor, he ran back the same way he had brought him.

However, the place the lad had run off from, and to which he had paid so little heed it might have been nothing, had the most unexpected effect on Victor. What mountain folk often call a 'col' is a sizeable mountain ridge that runs across between two higher peaks, joining them. As it always divides two valleys as well, it not infrequently happens that, when you are slowly climbing up from the one, without the least expecting it, you suddenly get the most surprising view down into the other. So it was here. The woods had opened out, the lake lay at the young man's feet and all the mountains he had seen from the plain and Attmaning were now ranged so peacefully, clearly and closely around the water that he imagined he could reach out and touch them—their rock faces, though, their ravines and crevices, were not grey but wreathed in a delightful blue, and the trees on them were like little sticks, or not to be seen at all on others, these latter ones stretching up heavenwards with perfectly smoothed sides.

Victor couldn't see a single house, a single person or animal. The lake that he had seen as a silvery streak from Attmaning was here broad and dark with not a single glint of light but mirroring rather the dusk of the screening walls that encircled it; and on the far shores were light objects reflected in the still waters which he could not identify.

Victor stood there for a while gazing out. He could smell the resin in the air but the air moved noiselessly through the pine forest. Nothing could be seen moving, if, that is, you discounted the further fading of the evening light, which was passing over the vaulting rock-faces, taking the colour-drained shadows with it.

There was in his heart almost a fear of this immensity that surrounded him here, and this drove him on to resume his journey. He walked down the path the lad had shown him. The mountains sank slowly into the forest, the trees took him into their embrace once more and, just as it had been on the col, when the flat lake had seemed, as it were, to push away the mountains it bordered, enabling the eye to take in the delicate gauze picture that projected itself from the green of the pine needles, so here, too, to his left, mountain and water now wove together a twilit picture up through the branches of the trees. And just as he had thought the climb up to the col would never end, so now the path dropped gently down seemingly forever. The lake was constantly to his left, and so near it seemed he might have been able to dip his hand into it, yet always just out of reach. Finally the last tree fell back behind him and he was standing down by the Afel again at the point where it left the lake and hurried away through sheer cliff faces, not leaving even a hand's breadth at its edge that might have made it possible to lay a path for travellers. Victor felt himself to be a hundred miles from Attmaning, it was so isolated here. There was nothing here but himself and the flat lake water, thundering ceaselessly into the Afel. Behind him stood the green silent forest, in front of him was the rippling expanse shut in by a blue mountain wall, which seemed to drop far down into the depths of the waters. The only work of man that he could see was the little footbridge that spanned the Afel and the specially constructed channel through which the water was forced to pass. He walked slowly over the footbridge followed by the dog, which was trembling and silent. Once across they were walking on ground that was grass-covered and next to high rocks. The place the boy had spoken of was soon recognisable: a whole lot of stones were lying around haphazardly and reaching out into the lake, so that it was easy to see a landslide had probably taken place. Victor turned a sharp corner of overhanging rock and immediately Hul lay in front of him: five or six grey cottages that stood on the shore of the lake not far off and were surrounded by tall green trees. The lake, too, which the overhang at the corner had earlier obscured, here lay spread out, and many mountains and rock faces which had hidden themselves from him came into view once again.

When Victor came to the houses he saw that they all had wooden extensions that projected out into the lake and beneath which lay moored-up boats. He couldn't see a church but on one of the cottages there was a little tower made of four posts painted red, between which a bell was hanging.

"Is there a place here called the Hermitage?" he asked an old man he found immediately sitting under the door lintel of the first cottage.

"Yes," replied the old man. "The Hermitage is on the island."

"Could you tell me who might take me across there?"

"Anyone in Hul could take you across."

"So, could you, then?"

"Yes—but they won't receive you there."

"I have an appointment at the Hermitage and I'm expected."

"That's different if you have business there and are expected. Are you coming straight back?"

"No."

"Wait here a moment, then."

At this the old man went into the cottage, returning soon, however, with a strong, rosy-cheeked young girl, who with bare arms set about pushing a boat further out into the water, while the old man put on his coat and fetched two oars. For Victor there was a wooden seat that had been fixed on the boat, and this he let himself down onto, setting his knapsack down next to him and holding the dog's head, who nestled up against his lap. The old man had taken up his position at the prow of the boat and facing the shore while the girl stood at the stern with the oar in her hand. The first stroke of the oars in the water came simultaneously from both, the boat thrust forward, slipped out into the smooth lake water and at every oar stroke sliced rhythmically through the darkening, trickling surface. Victor had never been on such a large stretch of water. The village retreated and the rock faces around the lake began moving very slowly. After a while a bush-covered spit of land came into view and grew in size in the water. Eventually this broke away completely from the land and was revealed to be an island. It was towards this island that the two rowers bent their oars. The nearer they came, the more clearly it rose up and the wider the space became that separated it from the land. Earlier a mountain had obscured it. At last very large trees could be made out on it, looking at first as if they were growing up out of the water, but then seen to be crowning a rocky shore of some height, whose sharp cliffs fell perpendicularly into the deep. Behind the greenery of these trees there drifted the gentle shape of a mountain, to which the evening light had given a charming blush.

"That's the Grisel on the far side of the lake," the old man said in answer to Victor's enquiry, "a mountain of some note but not that hard a climb. There's a path going over it to Blumau and Gescheid where the blacksmiths are."

Victor looked at the beautiful mountain, which drifted and sank into the foliage of the trees as they came nearer.

At last they reached the green water, where the mass of trees on the island plunged their reflection into the lake water, penetrating its depths. Then across from Hul the little bell hanging between the four posts rang out for evening prayers. The two rowers immediately shipped their oars and quietly said their evening prayers while the boat thrust forward as if of itself alongside the grey rocks that descended from the island into the lake. Here and there on the surrounding foothills the light played deceptively. The lake had even acquired stripes, some of which shone and even threw up flashes, even though the sun had set some while earlier. Across all this came the continuing and diligent ringing of the bell, rung by invisible hands as it were, since Hul could no longer be seen, and around the lake there was not one spot that even from a distance might have seemed like a human habitation.

"There must be a bell at the Hermitage cloister, too. A beautiful Angelus, I think," said the old man, after he had put his cap back on and picked up the oar, "but it's never rung; at least I've never heard its sound. You don't even hear the clock striking there. My grandfather said it was very beautiful in the past when all the pealing of the bells rang across the lake—for the monks were there then; it would ring across from there in the light morning mist without your knowing where it was coming from, for you'll have seen that we've come round the mountain now and that you can't see the island from Hul. That mountain is the high Orla and two monks once climbed over it when the snow was fathoms deep because the lake was frozen over but wouldn't have borne their weight and because they'd run out of provisions. With the servants they had in the boat they cut a pathway through the ice so that the boat could move, and when they came to the mountain they climbed over its summit down into Hul, for there's no footpath possible between the mountain and the lake. Well over a hundred years have gone by since then and it seldom happens that the lake is completely covered over with an ice sheet."

"So there were monks on the island once?" asked Victor.

"Yes," answered the old man. "Foreign monks came here in very ancient times when there wasn't a single house anywhere on the lake and nothing floated on it but a tree that had fallen down into it from the rocks. They went across to the island on rafts and pine trunks and built the hermitage first, from which the cloister slowly arose, and in later years Hul was built, too, where Christian folk fished the waters and went across to the Hermitage for mass; for in those days the lords of the land were out and out heathens and, with their cruel and savage squires, would slaughter those priests coming with the Cross as missionaries from Scotland. On finding the island, the brothers found safety, for you can easily see that those rocks descending there together form something like a fortress. It takes only a little wind to whip up such a foam here it's enough to swallow up any boat. There's only one spot where you can land, and that's where the rocks pull back, leaving a gap, and there the water flows inshore onto good sand. In this way the brothers were protected—just like the old man is, too, who chose to make the island his home. For this reason, also, people fish here only on very fine, calm days like today."

While the old man had thus been speaking, they had travelled gradually a good distance along the shore of the island and approached the place where the rocks are lower, forming a gentle, sandy bay that then rises up into sloping woodland. As soon as the rowers reached this spot, they immediately steered the tip of the boat into it, propelling it towards the sand. The old man got out, pulled the boat by the chain at the prow yet further towards dry land, so that Victor could disembark without getting his feet wet. The latter then stepped out over the prow and the dog sprang out after him.

"Now if you take that path, which you'll soon see up there," the old man said, "you'll come to the Hermitage. There's also a very sturdy boathouse on the island, in fact—on the shore that faces the Grisel—which the monks had built with wooden beams into the sloping cliffside to store their boats; but you can't get in that way because the wooden barricade is always locked. Now God bless you, young sir—and if you're not staying too long and the owner of the hermitage doesn't give you a boat for the return crossing, then just get old Christoph to let me know and I'll pick you up again from this spot. They at the Hermitage don't always have time to send out a boat."

Victor had meanwhile taken the agreed fare out of his small purse and handed it to the man, whereupon he said: "Goodbye, old friend, and if you'll allow, I'll call by at your house on my return and perhaps you can then tell me some more of your stories about the past."

He didn't venture to speak to the girl, who had been standing still all the while in the back of the boat.

But the old man replied: "Ah, and how could such a young and educated gentleman find pleasure in my stories, now?

"More than you think perhaps, and more than in those to be read in books," said Victor.

The old man smiled, as the answer pleased him; he didn't pursue the matter, though, but bent down, wound up the short chain, stowing it back into the prow, and got ready to leave.

"Well, God be with you, young sir," he concluded, gave the boat a shove with his foot, and jumped into it quickly, making it rock from side to side as it slid back into the water. After a few moments Victor could see the two oars rising and falling rhythmically as the boat thrust out across the mirroring water.

The shore rose up and it took him several steps to climb to the topmost edge, from where he could look far out over the lake. Gazing after the people in the departing boat, he said to his companion, as if the dog were a rational being and could understand his words: "I thank God that we have arrived at our journey's end. Whatever else may follow, the Lord has brought us here safe and sound."

He gave one last look out across the broad and beautiful surface of the lake, which in the fading light of evening was growing dark, then turned round and walked into the bushes towards the path in front of him.

At first it was uphill all the time through shrubbery and deciduous trees—but then the ground levelled out. The bushes had petered out and now there were only exceptionally large sycamore trees standing round about in a dark meadow as if according to a certain order and set of rules. It was clear to see that a good road had once run along here but it had become choked and shrunken with rank scrub everywhere. Victor walked through the strange sycamore garden, after which, passing through a fresh growth of bushes, he reached a curious place. It was like a meadow, on which there were small fruit trees, some of which were rotten. But in the midst of these trees in the grass was the round, stone lip of a well and all around between the trees stood grey stone dwarves holding bagpipes, lyres, clarinets and other kinds of musical instruments. Many were disfigured and there was no track or made-up path from one to the other; instead they stood there simply in the long, straggling grass. Victor looked at this strange world for a while and then toiled onwards. His path took him from this garden, down some old stone steps into a hollow and up again on the other side. There were bushes here like everywhere else but behind them

Victor saw a high windowless wall in which there was a iron grille and where the path ended.

Victor correctly concluded that this must be the entrance to the Hermitage and so approached the grille. On reaching it, he found it closed and there was no bell and no knocker. It was patently clear now that this was indeed the entrance to the house. Behind the iron grille was a levelled, sandy square on which flowers were growing. On the square was a house, but only the front part of this was visible—the rear was lost to sight behind bushes. Wooden steps led up into the first floor of the house directly from the sand square. On the other side of the square, bordered again with bushes, it was clear that the lake began once more, for behind the greenery was the fine, soft mist that likes to collect over mountain water, and, rising up, the Grisel with a pink glow on its rock face.

While Victor was thus looking looking in through the iron bars of the grille and trying in various ways to find a device which might open it, an old man stepped out of the bushes and looked towards Victor.

"Would you be so good," said the boy, "as to open the gate for me and take me to the master of this house, if this building is indeed called the Hermitage?"

The man said not a word in reply but instead came nearer, looked at Victor for a while and then asked: "Did you come on foot?"

"I came on foot as far as Hul," Victor replied.

"But is that really true?"

Victor went bright red, for he had never lied.

"If it were not," he answered, "then I wouldn't say so. If you are my uncle, as it would perhaps seem, I have a letter here from my guardian that states who I am and that I have covered the journey here on foot only at your express request."

With these words the youth pulled out the letter, which, as his foster-mother had recommended, he had kept clean, and reached it through the bars of the grille.

The old man took the letter and put it away unread.

"Your guardian is a fool and a man of limited ability," he said. "I can see that you look exactly like your father did when he started to get up to his tricks. I saw you already as you were coming across the lake."

Victor, who had never heard a callous word in his life, was struck dumb and waited simply for the other to open the gate.

The old man, however, said: "Take a rope and a stone and drown that dog in the lake, then come back here; I'll open up for you in the meantime."

"Whom should I drown?" asked Victor.

"That dog you brought with you."

"And if I don't?"

"Then I won't open the gate for you."

"Come, then, Pom," said Victor.

With this he turned round, ran down the steps into the hollow, climbed up the other side, ran through the dwarf garden, through the sycamore plantation, through the shrubbery beyond, and so reached the bay of the lake, shouting out with all the strength he could muster: "Boatman! Old man!"

But it was impossible for the old man to hear him. You wouldn't have been able to hear the crack of a rifle shot any more at that distance. The little boat stood out like a black fly against the dark promontory at the foot of Mount Orla that jutted out into the evening light of the lake. Victor took out his handkerchief, tied it to his staff and waved it back and forth every which way to attract attention. But no one saw him and finally, with him still waving, the black fly disappeared around the spit of land. The lake was completely empty and all that Victor could see, playing along the rocks of the island, was the soft flecking of the waters in the evening wind that had arisen meanwhile.

"It doesn't matter—it really doesn't matter," he said. "Come, Pom, we'll sit ourselves down in the bushes by the shore and see the night through there. Tomorrow a boat is sure to appear which we can wave over to us."

He was true to his word. He sought out a spot where the grass was short and dry and where there were thickly overhanging bushes but where he still had a good view of the lake.

"You see what a good thing it is," he said, "to put something by every morning. You're seeing the truth of this for the second time now on this journey."

At this he pulled out two bread rolls he had taken with him that morning at the inn by the river Afel and began to feed both himself and the dog with them. When this business was concluded, the traveller, who had believed he had reached his journey's goal, sat for the first time in the simple lodgings of the open air and looked at the objects around him. The mountains, the beautiful mountains he had so delighted in as he had approached, grew darker and darker and cast threateningly dark and splintered patches onto the lake, in which was still mirrored the pale gold of the evening sky, which now and then leapt up through the dark mountain reflections. And the objects round about him, wrapping themselves about in the shadows of the night, grew ever more strange. The lake was the colour of dross and pale gold and these were stirring and often intermingling, a sign that a gentle wind must have been getting up. Victor's eyes were accustomed of course only to the beautiful and lively impressions of the day, but he found himself unable to divert his gaze from this gradual draining away of colour from things and from the night's enshrouding peace. His limbs were so tired that sitting on the soft grass, protected by the bushes stretching over him, seemed very pleasant to him. He sat there with the dog next to him so long that eventually the darkness closed in with ever-increasing swiftness over lake, mountains and sky. He then decided to lie down. He fastened all the buttons of his coat, as his foster-mother had taught him, so as not to catch cold—round his throat he tied the neckerchief he had taken off during the day—he took out his waxed raincoat and put it over him—then he arranged the knapsack as a pillow and laid his head down, now that the darkness stood round him like a wall. Soon the urge to sleep spread through all his tired limbs where he lay. The bushes whispered in the gentle breeze from the lake which had wafted over to where he was, and the surf murmured distinctly from one rock face to the other.

74

His senses surrendered up to these ever-weakening impressions, and he was about to lapse into oblivion when he was awoken by a soft growling from the dog. He opened his eyes—a human shape was standing several steps in front of him close to the landing place, silhouetted darkly against the glittering water of the lake. Victor strained his eyes to see if he could recognise more from the shape but the outline revealed only that it was a man, whether young or old he was not able to ascertain. The figure was standing there very quietly and seemed to be looking fixedly out over the water. Victor raised himself to a sitting position and also remained quiet. On the dog growling again more loudly this time, the figure turned round suddenly and called out:

"Is that you there, young sir?"

"A young traveller with his dog is here," said Victor. "What do you want?"

"For you to come to dinner, for the mealtime is nearly over."

"For dinner? To whose dinner? And who is it you're looking for?"

"I'm looking for our nephew, for his uncle has been waiting for a quarter-of-an-hour already."

"Are you his companion—or his friend?"

"I am his servant and go by the name of Christoph."

"Of the master of the Hermitage, of my uncle?"

"Of the very same. He received notice of your landing."

"Then tell him," said Victor, "I intend to sit here the whole night and that I will rather hang a stone about my own neck and throw *myself* into the lake than drown the dog that is with me."

"I'll tell him that."

At this the man turned round and was about to leave.

Victor cried out after him again: "Christoph, Christoph."

"What do you want, young sir?"

"Is there no other house or cottage or anything else on the island where one could spend the night?"

"No, there's nothing here," the servant replied. "The old cloisters are locked, the church, too—the store rooms are crammed full of old tools and also bolted and barred—apart from that there's nothing."

"All right," said Victor. "I definitely won't be visiting my uncle's house—I won't be asking for shelter there. I think the old boatman who brought me across mentioned your name and said you sometimes went to Hul."

"I fetch our provisions and other things."

"Listen, then, I'll pay you handsomely if you ferry me back to Hul tonight."

"Even if you paid me far more than I would ask, it would be out of the question for three reasons. First, all the boats are in the log boathouse, the gate is locked and, what's more, every boat is chained up with a padlock round its crossbeam, to which I have no key. Secondly, even if there were a boat, no ferryman would take you. I'll tell you why. Do you see the white patches on the lake over there towards Mount Orla. Those are patches of mist, sitting almost on the rocks of the shore below the Orla. We call them 'the geese'. And if the geese are ever sitting in a row, then a mist is on the way. When the west-erly—that's the wind that comes out of the ravines down onto the lake after every sunset—when that stops blow-ing, then within half-an-hour the lake is full of mist and it's then impossible to know where to steer a boat. The mountain ridges run down into and under the water and are often barely submerged. If you ran into one of those and the boat sprang a leak, then you'd have to clamber out and wait in the water until someone saw you when it was light. But no one would see you because the fisher-men never come near those reefs. Do you understand what I'm saying, young sir?"

"Yes, I understand," Victor answered.

"And the third reason I can't take you across is because if I did I would be a disloyal servant. The master hasn't instructed me to take you to Hul, and if he doesn't do so, then I won't."

"All right," replied Victor, "then I'll stay sitting here until some vessel comes close enough tomorrow for me wave it over here to me."

"There aren't any vessels that come this near," replied the servant. "There's no trade route across this lake of ours because the only route that continues from the other shore is just a footpath over the Grisel and travellers wanting to get to this path travel from the shore opposite our island. Then there's so much surf round the shores of the island that fish are few and far between and fish-ermen rarely come this close. It could be eight days or more before you saw one."

"Then my uncle will have to get someone to take me

back to Hul tomorrow because he was the one who demanded I came here and I don't wish to stay here any longer," said Victor.

"He may do that," the servant replied, "I don't know, but right now he's waiting for you with supper."

"How can he be waiting," said Victor, "when he said I should drown my dog, when he said he wouldn't let me in if I didn't, and when he saw me then leave and didn't call me back?"

"I don't know about all that," Christoph answered, "but at the Hermitage your arrival was known about and the table was laid to include you. The master instructed me to call you because you don't know our mealtimes—he didn't say anything else. However, when he instructed me to call you, since I saw you leaving the grille entrance gate and running off the way you did, I immediately thought to come to this place, that I'd find you here. At first, when I couldn't see you, I fully thought you'd gone back across the water, but that wasn't possible of course—the man who brought you must have already gone round the Orla promontory by the time you got back here."

When Victor said nothing in reply to this, the man stood there for a short while and then said again: "The master is certain to have started eating by now, for he has his set times and sticks to them."

"That's of no consequence to me," replied Victor. "He can eat his fill, I want nothing from his table, for my dog and I have already eaten the bread that I put aside."

"Well, I must go and tell him that," the servant continued, "but you should consider, as you said yourself, that you came here because your uncle wanted you to, that he wants to talk to you and that you are the one making this impossible if you stay sitting here in the open air in the grounds of his house."

"I wanted to go to him," Victor rejoined, "I wanted to speak to him and greet him respectfully—my mother told me it was a good thing, and my guardian recommended it, too—but before I let any harm come to the animal that sought me out at great risk to himself and accompanied me here, I'd rather put up with injury and death myself."

"Nothing will happen to the animal," said Christoph. "The master was just giving you a piece of good advice; if you don't take it, it won't bother him unduly. He's clearly forgotten all about it, otherwise he wouldn't have sent me to fetch you for supper."

"If you can guarantee me that nothing will happen to the dog, then I'll come with you," said Victor.

"I can guarantee you that," replied the servant. "Such a trifle as a dog is now the last thing on his mind and he'll have no objection to it."

"Come on then, old Pom," said Victor, getting to his feet.

His hands appeared to tremble as he rummaged in his knapsack for a rope, which he always took with him, along with a variety of other things. This he tied to the ring on the collar the dog was wearing. He then shouldered his knapsack, picked his staff up from the ground and followed old Christoph, who took him the same route he had gone at dusk and when he had then run back again. It would have been difficult to find in the dark if old Christoph hadn't been leading the way. They passed through the bushes, through the sycamores, through the dwarf garden, across the broad hollow and so reached the iron grille gate. Christoph pulled a small object out of his pocket that Victor thought was a key, but it was a whistle, with which the servant blew a piercing sound. Immediately the gate was opened by unseen hands—to Victor's total incomprehension—and then closed behind them again with a clang. From the sandy forecourt, on which they now found themselves, Victor looked immediately towards the house. There was light coming from only three of the front windows, two upstairs and one on the ground floor—all the rest were dark. Christoph led the youth from the forecourt up the covered wooden steps, and so to the first floor. They came into a corridor, and from there into the room to which the two lit windows belonged. Here, and without another word, Christoph left the youth standing and backed out of the room. At the table Victor's uncle was sitting all by himself and eating. Earlier in the evening, when Victor had first seen him, he had been wearing a wide coat of grey cloth—he had removed this and was now in a wide dressing gown with a floral pattern and had on a red skullcap with gold edging.

"I'm on the crabs already," he said to the young man who had just entered. "You were too long in coming. I have my fixed times, as good health dictates, and I keep to them. They will bring you something in a moment. Sit down on the chair opposite me."

"My mother and guardian send you their greetings," Victor began, standing there still with his knapsack on his back and wanting to convey first his relations' messages and then his own respects and greetings.

His uncle, however, raised both his hands, each one of which held a piece of broken crab, and, gesturing back and forth, said: "I know who you are from your face—so your stay here, where I have summoned you, should now begin—and you are the one I summoned, that I acknowledge. We are at table now, so sit down and eat. As for what else needs to be done, that will happen in due course."

Victor therefore put his knapsack down on a chair, leant the walking staff in a corner and then made for the chair indicated, pulling the dog after him. The thin face of the old man he now sat opposite was bent down over his plate and took on a reddish hue as he ate. He broke open the crabs very adroitly with his hands, took out the meat and sucked the juice out of the shell of the main body and the knot of legs. The goodwill that the youth had brought with him in his heart felt suffocated and he sat silently opposite his relation, who continued equally silently with the business of eating. On the table stood several variously shaped and coloured tall bottles, in which there must have been a variety of wines; his uncle had probably already drunk from these, for next to every bottle there stood an accompanying glass with wine dregs at the bottom. Only one bottle was still standing next to the plate and from this the old man periodically poured himself out a few drops into a small wine glass which had a green bowl. In the meantime Victor was brought some soup, which he ate with his right hand, while with his left he held the dog sitting beneath him against his knee. While he was eating his soup, an old woman gradually carried in so many dishes for him that he was amazed. He ate until he had had enough and then left the rest where it stood. His uncle hadn't offered him any of the wines; Victor detested wine anyway and instead helped himself to the water from a fine crystal bottle that was replenished regularly by the same old woman who stood in attendance; he had never drunk such excellent, fresh and full-bodied strong water, he noted. While he was eating his fill, his uncle ate some cheese and then a variety of fruit and confectionery.

Thereupon the old man himself carried the various plates, with glass covers over the dessert items, and put them into cupboards set into the walls, locking them away. He then poured the wine dregs each back into its own bottle and locked the bottles away into similar cupboards.

In the part of the room where his uncle had sat during the meal a thick carpet was spread out and on this three fat old dogs were lying; the old man had occasionally thrown them first a crab claw, then an almond, then a piece of cake. The moment Victor had entered with his dog, all three of these had growled and during the meal, whenever he had passed a small piece of food down to his wretched dog, they had again curled their lips and whined feebly.

For as long as his uncle had been busy eating his dinner, he hadn't said a word to Victor, almost as if there weren't time for anything else; now, however, he said: "So you brought that bag of bones with you again after all. Whoever has an animal has to be able to feed it, too. I advised you to throw it into the lake but you thought better. I've never been able to abide students' dogs; they're like sad spectres. And it's precisely those types who insist on having dogs. Where did you pick it up? And did you bring it here without giving it anything to eat on the way?"

"It's my foster-mother's dog, Uncle," said Victor. "I didn't pick him up anywhere, neither bought nor exchanged; he ran after me, in fact, on the third day after I left. He must have run hard, something he wasn't used to doing before; he also must have been very frightened, something again he never had cause to feel with my foster-mother—and it's for this reason that in the days following he became so thin, thinner than he's ever been, even though I gave him whatever he wanted. Allow me then to keep him here in your house, so that I can return him to my foster-mother; otherwise I would have to journey back immediately and take him back to her."

"And so you've had it with you all the time, day and night?"

"Of course."

"So that he can rip open your throat one day."

"That he'd never do. It would never enter his head. He has lain down at my feet whenever I rested or slept, rested his head there, and he would rather starve than leave me or do me any harm."

"Give him something to eat, then, and don't forget water or he'll get foul-tempered."

When dinner had finished, the old woman had come in and out, taking out the dishes, plates and their lefto-vers; now Christoph came, whom Victor hadn't seen since he had brought him here.

On seeing the servant enter, his uncle said to him: "Make sure you lock them in the stall properly, so none of them can get out, but before that let them walk about a bit downstairs on the sand."

At this the three dogs got up, as if at a familiar sign. Two of them followed Christoph of their own accord, while the third he took by the scruff and dragged out.

"I'll show you your bedroom myself," his uncle said to Victor.

On this he went into the interior of the room where it was noticeably dark, because there was just the one light burning on the table. There from a stand, or from some other thing—it was impossible to see what—he took a candlestick, came forward again, lit the candle and said: "Now follow me."

Victor put one strap of his knapsack over one arm, grabbed his staff, pulled the dog by the rope lead and went after his uncle. The latter led him through the door and out into a corridor, in which ancient cupboards were ranged in rows, then into another corridor which stood at a right angle, and finally again into a third, which was closed off by an iron grille, which was shut. His uncle opened this, led Victor forward a few more steps, then opened a door and said: "Here are your two rooms."

The first of these Victor walked into was large, the second smaller.

"You can lock the dog in the neighbouring room so that he doesn't do anything to you," said his uncle, "and close the windows because of the night air."

Having said this, he lit the candle standing on the table of the first room and left without further ado. Victor heard him locking the grille door at the end of the passage, then the shuffle of slippers fading away until in the house a silence reigned like that of the dead. To convince himself that he had heard right as regards the grille door, Victor went out into the passage to check. It was indeed the case: the iron grille door had been locked.

"You poor man," thought Victor, "can you be afraid of me?"

Then he put the candle he had taken out into the passage with him back onto the table next to the bent pewter washbasin and stepped up to the large, barred window. There were two windows in fact, hard up against each other and set into a stone moulding. As one of these was standing open, Victor looked out through the iron bars into the night, and the weight that had, as it were, been pressing down on his soul began to ease. It was a pale night that returned his gaze, with few stars filling the sky. A small sliver of the crescent moon may have been behind the house, for Victor saw its weak light shining on the leaves of a tree in front of the house—but the mountains opposite appeared completely devoid of light. He immediately recognised the Grisel, which had been mentioned so many times that day. It stood there like a flat, black silhouette against the silver of the sky, broadening outwards a little, lower down, and there on its shoulder stood a star, hanging down like a man-made, star-shaped medal of some order.

Victor looked out for a long time.

"In which direction is my mother's valley," he thought, "and the dear, shining cottage between the dark bushes?" For he had lost his bearings as a result of all the many twists and turns of the path along the Afel and the criss-crossing passages of the house.

"The stars will be shining down there, too, the elder tree will be standing quietly and the water will be rippling along. Mother and Hanna will be sleeping or still sitting at table after supper with their work, and thinking of me or even talking about me."

There was, of course, water outside his window now, too, a much larger amount than the stream in his native valley, but he couldn't see it, for it was covered by a still, white mist, which terminated above in a horizontal and what seemed to be straight line.

"No one now is looking out of the bedroom where I slept, watching the gleams of light in the busy waters of the stream, the trees standing round about, or the hills with the meadows rising up their sides."

As he was thus looking out, a damp and very cold night wind stole in gradually through the windows, so Victor closed them, and, before going to bed, went to inspect the second room. It was like the first, except that it had no bed. A soot-stained picture looked down from a niche— the portrait of a monk. Victor closed the narrow window here as well and returned to his bedroom. All the time he had, without thinking, been leading the dog around with him by the rope; he now undid the knot round the ring, took off the collar and said: "Lie down where you want, Pom—neither of us is going to shut the other away."

The dog looked at him clearly as if to say that everything appeared strange to him and that he didn't know where he was.

Victor now was the one to bolt the door of his room; then he undressed. While doing this, it struck him that he had seen just three people in the whole house that evening—and that all three of them were old.

After saying his evening prayers, something he had done conscientiously from earliest childhood, he got into bed. For a while he let the light continue to burn on his bedside table, until his eyelids grew too heavy and his senses began to fade. Then he put out the candle and turned over towards the wall.

The dog settled himself as usual at the foot of his bed, did him no harm, and for both of them, exhausted as they were, the night passed in a flash.

V

ISLAND SOJOURN

W HEN VICTOR WOKE THE NEXT MORNING, he was shocked by the grandeur that presented itself to him. The Grisel stood across from where he was, sparkling and gleaming in all its crevices, and although at night it had appeared to be the highest mountain, higher ones now rose up on either side of it that he hadn't seen in the night and these were now shining down, a soft blue, revealing in many places patches of snow, tucked into the crevices like white swans. Everything shone and shimmered in a mêlée of light; tall trees stood in front of the house glistening with more moisture than he had ever seen on them; the grass was a mass of dewdrops; everywhere broad shadows were cast; and the whole spectacle appeared again in the lake, which, swept clean of every wisp of mist, lay there like the most delicate of mirrors. Victor had flung open his window and thrust his glowing face out between the iron bars. He was awestruck. The sharpest of contrasts was created by all this encircling profusion of light and colours alongside the surrounding deathlike silence in which these gigantic mountains stood. There wasn't a soul in sight, even in front of the house—only some birds twittered sporadically in the sycamore trees. What a chorus of morning sounds must be ringing out up there in those heights, but they went unheard because they were too far away. Victor stretched his head out as far as he could, so as to be able to look around. He could see a considerable part of the lake. Everywhere rock faces marched alongside it, and the young man was quite unable to make out the way he had come. The sun had risen, too, at quite another place than he had expected, that is, behind the house, and his windows were still in shadow, which made the light of the rock faces opposite even more intense. He was similarly wrong about the moon, which, to judge from its light, he had thought to be a narrow sickle at the most, for it was a half-moon that was still standing in the sky, inclining down towards the mountain peaks. Victor was not yet familiar with the effect of light in the mountains. What a flood of light would have to have fallen on those distant walls of rock to illuminate them as brightly as the church tower of his village, which had always reached up into the dark-blue night air so shimmeringly white and sharp in the moonlight. Although the sun had risen quite high already, the air that streamed into his windows, however, was still cold and damp, much more so than he was used to at home; but this didn't trouble him: rather he found it simultaneously so hard and raw that it stimulated all his vital spirits.

He stepped back finally from the window and began to unpack his knapsack in order to put on something different from what he had had on for the journey, for today, he thought, his uncle would speak to him and explain why he had got him to come to this solitary island to see him. He laid out some clean clothes, brushed the dust from his second suit, which he had brought with him along with his travelling clothes, making full use of the crystal-clear water there in the pewter jug to wash the stains of the journey from himself; he then dressed in clothes that both went together and suited him, just as he had learnt to do in his foster-mother's spick-and-span house. He even combed and brushed the dog, who was such an unwelcome guest in this house. He then put his collar on again and tied the rope to its ring. When they were both completely ready, he opened his door and was about to set off for the room where they had eaten the evening before in order to find his uncle, when, in the passage, it struck him that he had forgotten to say his morning prayers that day for the first time. It must have happened as a consequence of the huge and un-precedented impressions he had been affected by that morning. He returned to his room, therefore, went and stood at the window again and spoke the simple words he had once secretly thought up for this purpose, and which no one knew anything about. Then he set off a second time in search of his uncle.

The iron grille door in the passage was no longer locked; he went through it and easily found the passage leading from the dining-room, out of which he had been led the evening before; but there was no door in the pas-sage that might have led into a room; instead, there were all these old cupboards that he had seen by candlelight the previous night. The windows in the corridor were boarded up from top to bottom; there was only a small opening left at the very top that enabled the light to peer in through the pane, as if his uncle feared the freedom and clarity of light, loving rather to have these passages in darkness. As Victor was thus looking around, the old woman who had brought in the dishes for dinner the night before stepped out of one of the cupboards. She was carrying cups and bowls and disappeared again into another of these same cupboards. When Victor looked more closely at the one she had come out of, he discovered that it was in fact a secret door casing, at the back wall of which was the door through which he had come the previous evening when going into his uncle's room; this he recognised from the ring and door knocker he'd seen picked out by the light the night before. He rapped softly on the knocker and on hearing a noise within that sounded like "Come in", he opened it and went in. He found himself indeed in yesterday's dining room and there beheld his uncle.

The only reason why all these similar-looking cupboards—dating perhaps from former times—seemed to have been placed in the passageway was so that anyone with dishonest intent wanting to go in through a door would not be easily able to realise this intent, since he would have to waste precious minutes examining real and false door frames. It was apparently for this same reason of greater security that the corridors had, in addition, been made dark.

His uncle was today dressed in the broad, grey coat that Victor had seen him in the day before when he had stood at the iron grille gate. He was standing now on a stool, holding a stuffed bird, which he was dusting off with a brush.

"I'll give you the house timetable today that Christoph has written down, so that you can act accordingly, since I've had to have breakfast already because it was time," he said to Victor as he entered, without any other morning greeting or welcome.

"I wish you a very good morning, Uncle," said Victor, "and apologise for not coming for breakfast at the right time—I didn't know when it was."

"Of course not, you fool—you couldn't have known, and no one asked you to. Pour out some water for the dog in that wooden trough."

On so saying, he stepped down from the stool, walked over to a stepladder, climbed it and put the bird in the top compartment of a glass cupboard, taking out another in place of this and beginning to dust this one, too.

Now in the light of day Victor could see how unusually gaunt and decrepit the man was. Nothing suggesting goodwill and sympathy was conveyed by his features, which were instead turned in on themselves, as with someone on the defensive, someone who for countless years has loved only himself. His coat hung loosely round his arms and his reddish, shrivelled neck protruded up from the collar. His hair, though still not completely grey but made up of a mixture of many jarring colours, hung untidily around his shrunken temples, and never, from the time it first grew, had it been stroked by a loving hand. His eyes, which started out from under his drooping brow, were fixed on the tiny contours of the dead bird. The upper edge of his coat collar was very dirty and part of his shirt that was bulging out from the sleeve was also dirtier than any he had ever seen at his foster-mother's home. And all about the man were things that were either lifeless or decayed. And in the room were a host of stands, shelves, nails, deer antlers, and all these had something hanging from them and something standing on them. Everything was, however, so strictly guarded that dust lay everywhere, many of the things not having been moved from their place for years. Dust clung to the insides of the dogs' collars, a whole bundle of which were hanging up; the folds of the tobacco pouches had fossilised rigid from being untouched an unimaginably long time; the stems in the collection of pipes were all split open, and the pieces of paper underneath the countless paperweights had yellowed. The room, which, instead of having a ceiling, was very steeply vaulted, had originally been painted but the tones and shades of this colour had drained away into a uniform, ancient grey. A faded carpet lay on the floor and only there, where the man would sit at mealtimes, was a newer, smaller one laid, which had fresh colours. Right now the three dogs were lounging on it. Standing in this old man's room, Victor presented a very striking contrast: an almost virginal innocence blossomed on his handsome face, which was full of strength and joie de vivre, framed neatly by his evenly dark hair, and, as he stood there in his suit, he was so cleanly turned out that it seemed he had just at that moment been attended to by the loving hands of a mother.

He stood still, just as he had on entering the room, and looked at his uncle. The latter, however, continued what he was doing as if no one were present. He must have neglected to do this for a very long time and had set about it at first light, for already a fair number of birds had been cleaned, while the rest still stood there behind their glass panes, quite grey with dust. The old woman, who had crossed Victor's path earlier without saying anything to him, now brought in a tray of breakfast and set it down, again without a word, on the table. Victor concluded it was for him, since it had been brought in on his arrival. He sat down therefore and ate as much as he was used to doing in the morning, for there was far more on the tray than he needed. It was like the customary English breakfast, beginning with tea and coffee and followed by eggs, cheese, ham and cold roast beef. The dog was the one who benefited most, for Victor gave him more than he had perhaps ever received before in the morning.

"Have you put some water in the trough?" his uncle asked.

"No," replied Victor. "It slipped my mind a moment, but I'll do it now."

The young man, while looking at his uncle, had in reality forgotten what the latter had wanted him to do. He therefore took the large glass jar standing on the table with the same wonderful water it had had yesterday and poured some of it into a small, well-polished wooden trough that was on the floor by the wall next to the door. After Victor's dog had drunk his fill, his uncle left his work and called his dogs over to the water, but since none of them showed any interest, probably because they had already been given water anyway, his uncle pushed down on a lever protruding from the wall by the trough, at which a metal panel opened in the bottom of the trough, allowing the liquid to run away. Victor almost had to laugh at this device, for where he lived everything was conducted in a much simpler and homelier way: the dog was free to roam outside, drank from the stream and ate his food under the apple tree.

"I'll show you the picture of your father sometime perhaps," his uncle said, "so you can see how I immediately knew who you were."

Having said this, the old man climbed up the stepladder again and took out another bird. Victor continued to stand there in the room, waiting for his uncle to begin to talk about the reason for his coming there. But the latter failed to do so and carried on instead cleaning his birds. After a while he said: "Lunch is at exactly two o'clock. Set your watch according to the one over there and be here then."

Victor was taken aback and asked: "So you don't want to speak to me any more until then?"

"No," replied his uncle.

"Then I'd like to go outside, so as not to disturb you in what you're doing, and have a look at the lake, the mountains and the island."

"Do anything you want," his uncle said.

Victor hurried out but found the door leading out to the wooden steps locked. So he went back to his uncle and asked whether he might have it opened.

"I'll open it for you myself," the latter said.

He put the bird down, went out with Victor, pulled a key out of his grey coat, opened the door to the wooden steps with it and immediately locked it again after the youth.

Victor ran down the steps to the sandy forecourt. He was so dazzled by the delightful flood of light that met him here that he turned round a little in order to look at the house from the outside. It was a solid, dark building with just the one upper floor in which he had slept that night. He recognised his room by its open windows, for all the others were closed and also weather-worn, which lent them a variety of beautiful colours. They all had strong and solid iron bars in front of them. The main entrance door was blocked up and the covered wooden steps down to the sandy forecourt seemed to be the only way in. How different it was from home, where window after window stood open, in which soft white curtains swayed and where, from the garden, you could see the flickering of the cheerful kitchen fire!

Victor now turned his eyes towards the open ground leading away from the gloomy house. Of all the sur-rounding area it was the most welcoming. Behind him and at either side of the house it had tall trees; then it was strewn with sand, had here and there little benches, several flower beds, and, going down towards the lake, opened out into a proper flower garden and then into an area of bushes. Trees and shrubs grew on both sides. Victor walked around here and the air and sunshine did him good.

He then pressed on further to see what else there was to see. He had been struck by an ancient avenue of lime trees that led away from his uncle's house. The trees were so high and dense that the earth beneath them was damp and the grass tinted the most beautiful, delicate green.

Victor set off down the middle of this avenue. He came
to another building with a high, broad door, which was
locked and rusted up. Above the arch of the door carved
in stone were the symbols of spiritual power, staff and
mitre, alongside the other coats of arms of the place. At
the foot of this arch and below the whole length of the
wooden door soft, thick grass grew, a sign that no human
foot had trodden there for a long while. Victor saw he
couldn't get into the building through this door and so
he walked along the outside and took a close look at it.
The walls of the building formed an ash-grey square and
it had a tiled, almost black roof. The trees of the island
had run wild and grown high over it. The windows had
bars but behind most of these were not panes of glass
but boards washed grey by the rain. There was indeed
another small door into the building but, like the main
entrance, this, too, was blocked up. Further back was a
high wall, which probably enclosed the whole complex
of buildings and gardens, the entrance to which was
through his uncle's iron grille gate. In a salient angle of
this wall were the cloister gardens, from which vantage
point Victor could see the two thick but unusually short
towers of the church. The fruit trees were very neglected,
many of them being broken and half fallen. In marked
contrast to this mournful past was the burgeoning and
eternally young present that stood everywhere round
about. The high rock faces of the mountains, along with
their bright morning colours, looked down on the green
island, with its covering of trees and plants, and the
peace these emanated was so great and overriding that

97

the dilapidated building, this footprint of an unknown human past, amounted to only a small grey dot, unworthy of note in the budding and thrusting life all around. The dark tree tops were already overshadowing it, creepers were climbing the walls, their nodding heads peering in, below lay the flashing lake and on every height the rays of the sun cavorted in a display of glittering gold and silver.

Victor would dearly have liked to have walked the whole length of the island, which couldn't have been large and which he would have liked to have explored, but he was persuaded that the former cloisters along with all its side buildings and gardens really were, as he had assumed, ringed about by a wall, even though its stones were often hidden from sight by flowering shrubs. He returned to the sandy forecourt once again. Here he stood a good while in front of the grille gate, examining the bars and trying the lock. But to go up to his uncle and ask him to have it opened—this he couldn't bring himself to do, so reluctant did he feel—apart from the two old servants, the aged Christoph and the old woman, the whole building seemed like a morgue. He therefore abandoned the gate and from the open forecourt wandered straight ahead towards the lake in order to look down at the water from the rocky bank, should there be a bank there, too. There was, and, standing on its outermost edge, he found it to be as high as a house, in fact. Below him the water gently fringed the shore; opposite stood the Grisel with its inviting foothills, whose white rocks and other gleaming objects were mirrored in the water. And on looking around him at the mountain walls, beneath which lay the dark, motionless and flat water, he had the impression of being in a prison, of being somewhere that should almost inspire fear in him. He looked to see if he could find a place from which he could climb down to the water but the rock face, whipped by rain and storm, was as smooth as iron and curved inwards towards the water like an arch. How huge the rock faces of the Grisel must be, thought Victor, looking as they do from here like palaces reaching skywards, while the rocky shore of this island looked like a mere strip of sand, when we approached it.

After standing there for a while longer, he walked the length of the rocky cliff-edge that would bring him to the cloister side of the perimeter wall. When he reached this, the wall dropped perpendicularly down to the water. Then, turning round, he returned along the edge of the cliff towards the wall on the side opposite the cloister. But before reaching this, he came across something else. The ground there sank down, forming a hollow opening which was walled about and looked like the door of a cellar, and further into this he could indeed see steps going down. Victor thought these could be steps leading down to the lake, for fetching water perhaps. He immediately set off down this, into what indeed resembled the vaulted descent to a cellar, consisting of a seemingly endless number of steps. In this way he really did reach the water, but how astonished he was to behold, not a humble watering place, such as might be needed for the watering of plants perhaps, but instead a veritable water hall. Emerging from the darkness of the flight of steps, he saw two side walls, built of large square stones, reaching out towards the lake with stone ledges on either side that you could walk along next to the surface of the water, this forming, as it were, the floor of the hall. Above was a solid roof; the walls had no windows, and all the light there was came from the lake through a grille barricade made of very strong oak beams. The fourth, that is, the back wall, was formed by the rock face of the island itself. There were many stakes driven into the ground and several boats were moored to these by means of iron padlocks. The whole space was very large and must have once housed many such boats, to judge from the greatly worn appearance of the iron mooring rings on the stakes; but now there were only four there, which were fairly new, very well-built and attached to chains with locked padlocks. There were several gates set in the barricade to enable access to the lake, but they were all locked and the vertical beams of the barricade plunged deep down into the water and out of sight.

Victor stood still and looked out into the glittering green lights of the lake that appeared between the black oak beams. He then sat down after a while on the edge of a boat in order to test the warmth of the water with his hand. It wasn't as cold as he had supposed from its transparent clarity. Swimming had been one of his favourite pastimes since he was a child. On hearing, therefore, that his uncle's house was on an island, he had taken his swimming costume along with him in his knapsack, so he could pursue this sport as often as possible. He remembered this now in this boathouse and began looking for places where he might swim in future, but realised immediately that this was impossible, for where the boats were moored it was too shallow, while where it was deeper the beams of the barricade went down into the water. There was also no prospect of being able to get through the beams, for they were so close together that not even the slimmest body could have squeezed through. There was nothing for it, therefore, but to reserve this boathouse as somewhere he could just have a wash.

This intention he partly carried out straight away. He took off as many items of clothing as was necessary in order to wash some parts of his body, namely his shoulders, his chest, arms and feet. He washed the dog as well. Then he put his clothes back on and went back up the steps he had come down. Having then resumed his walk along the cliff edge, he came across the other end of the perimeter wall. This, like the other one, dropped down sheer into the water and was built out from the rock in such a way that a rabbit could barely have managed to slip round its edge. Victor stood idly at this place for a while—then his day's work, so to speak, was done. He went back to the sandy forecourt and sat down on a bench to rest after his wash and to dry the dog. His uncle's house, now opposite him, was as it had been in the morning. Only the windows of the room he had slept in were open, because he himself had opened them; all the rest were closed. No one came out, no one went in. The shadows slowly shifted and the sun, which had shone behind the house in the morning, now lit up the front. As he sat there looking at the dark walls, Victor felt as if he had already been away from his home for a year. Finally the hour hand of his watch pointed to two. So he got to his feet and climbed up the steps; on knocking on the door at the top he was let in by his uncle, who went ahead of him into the dining-room where they both immediately sat down at the table.

The midday meal was different from the previous evening's dinner only insofar as uncle and nephew ate together. Otherwise it was the same. His uncle said little, or next to nothing, in fact; the dishes were varied and good. Again several wines stood on the table and his uncle even offered Victor some—if he drank wine, that is. Victor declined the offer though, saying that he had always drunk water up till now and wanted to continue that way. His uncle didn't speak about the purpose of Victor's journey that day either, but instead, when the meal was over, got up and busied himself with a number of things in the room, where he rummaged about. Victor realised immediately that he was free to go and so, following his inclination, went out into the open air.

Later in the afternoon the heat in this valley basin, like the chill in the morning, was extreme, and as Victor was crossing the flower garden, he saw his uncle sitting on a bench in a full patch of sunlight. But the latter didn't call him over and Victor didn't go over to him either.

Thus ended the first day. Dinner, which the appointed hour of nine summoned him to, concluded for him as it had the day before. His uncle led him to his rooms and locked the iron grille door after him.

Victor hadn't seen old Christoph all day, only the old woman, who had waited on them at table—if bringing in and taking out dishes could in fact be called 'waiting on'. Everything else his uncle had done, including locking away the wine and cheese again.

When breakfast was over the next morning, he said to Victor: "Come in here a moment."

At this he opened a concealed door, barely recognisable as such, in the dining-room wall and stepped into the next-door room, into which Victor followed him. The room was sparsely furnished and contained more than a hundred firearms displayed in glass cabinets according to type and period. Hunting horns, game bags, powder containers, shooting sticks and a thousand other suchlike things lay around. They went through this room, then through the next, which again was bare, and then came into a third, in which there were some old objects. On the wall a single picture was hanging. It was round like the shields on which coats of arms used to be painted and was encircled by a broad and glittering gold frame, which was cracked with age.

"That's a painting of your father, whom you closely resemble," his uncle said.

A fine-looking young man in the bloom of youth—more a boy still, properly said—was portrayed on the circular plaque wearing a baggy brown suit decorated with gold braid. The painting, though no great masterpiece, was nevertheless endowed with that precision and depth of treatment which we often see in family portraits of the last century. Now superficiality and crude colouring have gained the upper hand. The gold borders were particularly finely executed, still glinting with sombre lights and standing out in fine relief from the snow-white, powdered wig and the sweet face, whose shadows were particularly pure and transparent.

"In that school for the sons of noblemen it was the foolish custom," said his uncle, "for all pupils to have their portraits painted as mementoes, and, in such round plaques, these would then be hung up in a number of places, in the corridors, the entrance halls and even in the main rooms. The pupils themselves bought the frames for them. Your father was always vain and had himself painted. I was much more good-looking than him and I didn't sit for one. When the school closed down, I bought the picture for here."

Victor had no recollection of his father, nor of his mother, for they had both died—first his mother and then very soon after his father—when he was very little. Now he stood in front of the picture of the one to whom he owed his life. A feeling gradually entered the soft heart of the youth, the feeling that orphans may often have when, while others have their parents standing before them in the flesh, they stand in front of mere pictures of them. It is a feeling rich with deep melancholy and yet one that also gives some bitter-sweet comfort. The picture was a reminder of a time long gone when the subject had still been happy, young and full of hope, just as the boy looking at it now was still young and brimful of limitless optimism for this world. Victor couldn't picture this same man as he may have looked later as he stood by his cradle in a dark, simple coat and with a haggard, careworn face. Even less could he imagine him then lying on his sickbed and how, when he was dead and as white as his shroud, he was put in a narrow coffin and lowered into the grave. All that had come to pass long before, when Victor was not yet aware of the impressions of the outer world, or wasn't able to retain these beyond one hour. He now stared up at the unusually charming, open and carefree face of the boy and thought that, if he were still alive, he would now be old, too, like his uncle—but he couldn't imagine him *looking* like his uncle, that he couldn't imagine. As he continued to stand there awhile, the decision arose in him that, should he find himself on better terms with his uncle than now, he would put forward the request that his uncle make him a gift of the picture, for it surely couldn't mean that much to him, having it here as he did in this untidy room, where it hung all alone on the wall, its frame gathering dust.

His uncle stood meanwhile to one side, looking at the picture and the youth. He had shown no special concern, and when Victor made the first move away from the picture, he immediately went on ahead so as to lead him out of the room, saying nothing more either about the picture or Victor's father other than the words: "The likeness is amazing."

Once back in the dining-room, he carefully closed the concealed door and began to walk about the room in his usual fashion, fiddling about with the objects lying and standing around—from which Victor deduced from

experience that his uncle no longer wished to have anything more to do with him for the present.

He therefore decided to go outside again onto the
island. The door to the outside steps was once again
closed. Victor didn't want to go to his uncle to get him
to let him out, but thought instead of the cupboard into
which the old woman had gone with the dishes the day
before and assumed there was a way out of the house
through there. He soon found the cupboard, opened it
and did indeed see steps leading down, but, on going
down these, instead of finding himself outside, they
brought him into the kitchen, where he met none other
than the old woman, who was busy with all the many
and various things to do with the midday meal. She was
being helped, however, by a girl who looked almost like a
simpleton. Victor asked the woman if she could let him
out into the garden.

"Of course," she said, led him back up the steps he
had come down and fetched his uncle, who immediately
opened the door for him and let him out.

Victor now realised that the wooden steps constituted
the only way out and that a deep distrust kept this sole
exit locked, even though the whole place was girt about
with an impenetrable wall.

The day passed like the day before. Victor came for
lunch at two o'clock and then went off again. Towards
evening something unusual took place. Victor saw a boat
coming towards the island and heading directly for the
wooden boathouse he had discovered the day before.
Victor ran hurriedly down the steps to the mooring

hall. The boat approached, the barred gate was opened from outside with a key, and old Christoph, quite on his own, rowed in. He had fetched provisions and other necesssities and for this reason had been in Hul and Attmaning. Seeing the cargo, Victor couldn't grasp how the old man could have put together such a load of things and rowed it all across the lake. He was also upset he hadn't been told about the old servant's trip, as he would have given him a letter that was to go to his mother. Christoph began to unload everything and, with the help of the simple girl, to carry the various sorts of meat on a litter up to the ice cellar. Victor saw them open a small and very low iron door at the rear of the house. When he went down the steps on the other side of this door, there, by the light of the lantern they had lit, he saw a huge pile of ice, on which all manner of provisions were lying, and which spread a dreadful chill throughout the room. The business of unloading was completed in the late dusk.

The third day passed in a similar way to the first two—and so, too, the fourth and the fifth, while in the distance the Grisel was a constant presence, with the bluish rock faces to the right and the left, while below lay the glimmering lake and, in the midst, the bright green of the island's mass of trees; and like a small grey stone in this green sat the monastery with the house. In the branches of the trees many a patch of blue from Mount Orla shone through.

Victor had now been in every place along the perimeter wall, had sat on all the benches in the sandy forecourt or garden, and stood on all the promontories along the shore's edge of that enclosed place.

On the sixth day he could not bear the way things were any longer and so decided to bring the matter to an end.

Early in the morning he dressed more carefully than usual and so appeared at breakfast. When this was over and he was standing in the room beside his uncle, he said: "Uncle, I wished to speak with you, if, that is, you have the time to listen."

"Speak," said his uncle.

"I would like to request that you kindly reveal to me the reason why I was obliged to come to this island, if, that is, you had a particular reason, for tomorrow I am going to resume my journey."

"It's more than six weeks still before you are to take up your post," his uncle replied.

"Not as long now, Uncle," said Victor. "Only thirty-five days. But I'd like to spend some time in my future place of residence before I take up my post and would therefore like to leave tomorrow."

"But I'm not letting you go."

"But if I ask you, and request that you have me taken over to Hul tomorrow, or, if you prefer, the next day, then you will let me go," said Victor firmly.

"I'll let you go only on the day you have to leave in order for you to arrive at your post in good time," his uncle rejoined.

"But you can't do that," said Victor.

"Indeed I can," his uncle replied, "for the whole property is surrounded by a strong wall dating back to the monks, the way out being the iron grille gate that no one besides me knows how to open, while the rocky shore of the lake, which forms the next border, is so steep that no one can get down to the water."

From childhood Victor had never been able to bear the least injustice and had clearly used the word 'can' in its moral sense, while his uncle had used it in its material sense; so on these last words his whole face became suffused with the dark red of indignation, and he said: "So I am a prisoner, then?"

"If you want to call it that, and if the way I have disposed things here makes it such, then you are," his uncle retorted.

Victor's lips now trembled and he was so agitated he couldn't say a word—but then he cried out: "No, Uncle! You cannot dispose things just as you would like, for I shall go down to the rocky lake shore, throw myself off and so be smashed to pieces."

"Do so, if you are that weak," said his uncle.

Now Victor really couldn't bring himself to utter another syllable—he was silent for a while and thoughts of revenge against the harshness of this odious man rose up in him. On the other hand he also felt ashamed of his childish threats and realised that by hurting himself he wouldn't be putting up a very effective resistance. He therefore decided to defy him with patience. And so it was he said finally: "And when the day you named comes, you'll then have me taken across to Hul?"

"I'll then have you taken across to Hul," his uncle replied.

"Good—well, I'll stay until then," Victor answered, "but I tell you, Uncle, that from now on all ties between us are severed and that we can no longer be on the same footing as relatives."

"Very well," replied his uncle.

Still in the room, Victor put his hat on his head, and, pulling the dog he had with him by his lead behind him, left the room.

The young man now regarded himself free of every obligation he had otherwise believed he was under as regards his uncle, and decided to give himself free rein to behave from now on in any way not forbidden by his sense of morality or made impossible by the limitations that blatant force now imposed on him.

Leaving his uncle, he went to his room and wrote there for over two hours. He then went outside. On either side of the door that opened out to the outer steps was a ring that served as a knocker. Whenever Victor from now on wanted to go out or come in, he no longer, as before, went to his uncle to get him to open the door for him, but instead stood there by the door and banged on it with the knocker. At this sign his uncle always came, if he was in his room, and opened up. If he was himself outside, then the door stood open anyway. During lunch this first day Victor said nothing, neither did his uncle ask him anything, and when the meal was over both of them got up and Victor left immediately. Dinner was the same.

Victor now set about investigating every part of the enclosure. He plunged into the shrubbery behind the house, went from one tree to the next, looking at and examining the features and form of each and every one. On one occasion he beat a path through all the bushes and creepers growing on the inside of the whole length of the property's perimeter wall. As musty and dilapidated as it was in many places because of the innumerable plants growing on it, the wall was everywhere nevertheless sound and solid enough. He also explored everything in the house in which he lived with his uncle, upstairs and downstairs and along every passage, but little came to light as a result of such investigations. At every point where a door or gate appeared, the padlocks were firmly in place, and large, heavy cupboards, which may once have contained cereals or suchlike, were standing in front of them, permanently preventing access, just as most of the windows in the passages, as Victor had immediately noticed the first day, were boarded up apart from a thin strip through which the light came. Except for the passages running between the dining-room and his two rooms, and the stairs which took him down to the kitchen—these two being areas he had been familiar with for some time—he discovered nothing in his uncle's house, apart perhaps from the stairs that had once led down to what had been the front door, but which now came to an end at a low gate, locked and covered in rust.

What gave Victor most pleasure was the old monastery. He walked round all the sides of the grey, desolate square building, and one day, when he was in the tumbledown cloister garden, from which the church towers were visible, he managed to climb over a low transverse wall, from which he was able to break off several tiles, and so into an outer courtyard, and from there into unlocked rooms inside. He walked through a passage where the old abbots had gone in and out, and where their portraits looked down from blackened pictures, with their names and dates in blood-red at the foot of each. He came into the church and stood in front of the altars, stripped of their gold and silver—then, crossing many flagstones worn smooth by countless footsteps, he had reached some cells, whose doors happened to be open, and which now echoed in the musty air. Finally he had climbed up the towers and seen the silent, dust-laden bells hanging there. After climbing back over the diagonal wall into the orchard, he released his dog, which he had tied up to a trunk, and left.

Several days after the strange scene with his uncle, he went down to the boathouse in order to wash himself partially in the refreshing water, as he had often done now. As he was sitting on the bottom step in order to cool off, and looking in front of him, he noticed in the depths of the water, either because it was a particularly fine day or because he had become more observant, that one of the pointed stakes of the barred outer gate reaching down into the water was shorter than the others, and so made a gap through which it might be possible to dive down through and so reach the lake outside. He decided to attempt it immediately. To this end he went to his room and fetched his swimming costume. On returning with this and having cooled off and changed, he headed for the deeper part of the water; there he laid himself along the surface, dived under carefully, swam forwards, lifted his head up and found himself outside the barricade. After taking off his lead, he was even able to take the dog out with him through the struts, being as thin as he was. The boy now swam around happily in the deep lake in large circles away from and back to the barricade, with his dog paddling alongside him. When he had exercised himself enough, he approached the gap again, dived, went under the stakes and so back into the boathouse. After this swim he dressed and left. He now did this every day. When the heat of the day started to ease off, he went to the boathouse, got himself ready and then swam as long as he pleased outside and around the barricade.

At this time the idea struck him that he could get his clothes out through the barricade stakes along with a store of bread and pull these along behind him floating on a rope, until he had swum round the nearest end of the wall that curved inland. He could climb out there, dry his clothes off in a hidden place and then put them on. It would surely be possible, if only the bread held out, to wait there until he could get one of the little boats fishing on the lake to come over and pick him up. Indeed, in moments when his imagination was most fired, he even had the idea that, drawing hard on his physical strength and summoning all his spirits, he could perhaps swim over as far as Mount Orla—from there he would have to find his way, by climbing and hiking, over to Hul. The enormity of this piece of daring didn't seem so daunting to him, because after all the monks had once climbed over Mount Orla, too, and that was in winter as well.

But he didn't stop to think that the monks were men who knew the mountains, while he was but a youth who had no experience of these things. But as enticing as all these delusions may have been, he couldn't carry any of them through, since he had promised his uncle to stay there until the requisite day—and he wanted to keep this promise. For this reason he always came back under the barricade after his swim.

Apart from swimming he spent the rest of his time doing other things. He had already visited and familiar-ised himself with each and every corner of the enclosure area. He now began to pay attention to the coming and going of the lights on the mountains and little by little became aware of the quivering colours that passed over them as the times of day slowly changed or when the clouds raced faster over the bright overarching sky. Or, while sitting with the sun at its zenith or when it had just dipped behind the mountain ridge, he would listen to see if he could hear the bell from Hul ringing for prayers—for on the island you could hear neither the striking of the hour from a clocktower nor the tolling of a bell: but he never heard anything, for the green and thick wall of trees that covered the best part of the island lay between his ears and the beautiful sound he had heard on that first evening on the lake, coming from the rocky shore. After a long period of starry nights—for Victor had arrived when the moon was waning—very beautiful moonlight nights had finally made their appearance. Victor then liked to open his windows and, being cut off from his fellow man, watch the magical light shimmering, glittering and fading on the lake and rock faces, and then see the black, unlit rock masses in the midst of this sparkling world, hovering like strangers.

He spoke not a word to Christoph and the old woman servant whenever they met him, since he didn't think it proper to exchange words with his uncle's servants when he was not speaking to their master.

And so the time slowly passed.

One day towards five o'clock, as he was crossing the flower garden on his way to the boathouse for a swim, with his poor dog as usual on a lead behind him, his uncle, who was sitting as was his wont on a bench in the sun, addressed him and said: "You don't have to have the dog on a lead like that. You can let him run free with you if you want."

Astonished, Victor looked in the man's direction and saw no dishonesty at least in his face, though nothing else besides.

The next afternoon he tried letting his dog go. Nothing happened to him and from now on he let him off the lead every day.

And so again more time passed.

On another occasion, when Victor was in the middle of a swim and happened to raise his eyes, he saw his uncle standing and looking down at him from a door that opened from the roof of the boathouse. The expression on the old man's face seemed to suggest an appreciation of the skill with which the youth cut through the water and of how he often looked fondly at the dog swimming alongside him. The great beauty of the youth, too, spoke gently in his favour, how the water played about his young limbs and flowed round his innocent body, abiding the ravaging might of time and what fate had in store in the unfathomable future. Whether in the old man there were also some feelings of kinship stirring towards the young person, the only one who stood closer to him in blood than any other in the world—who can tell? Whether today was the first time he had watched him or whether he had done so often already, was also not certain, for Victor had never before looked up towards this door in the boathouse roof. But the next day, at five in the afternoon when Victor was crossing the garden and saw his uncle tending the flowers, the only loving activity he had ever seen him engaged in, and had walked by without saying anything to him, he found to his great astonishment, when he had reached the boathouse, one of the barricade doors standing open. He was inclined to attribute this event to some circumstance unknown to him; but at five o'clock the next day and on every day that followed the boathouse stood open, while for the rest of the entire day it was always locked.

These things put Victor on the alert and he quickly realised he was being watched by his uncle.

The time passed so deathly slow that one day he found himself standing yearningly at the iron grille gate of the perimeter wall once more—something which out of pride he had never done since his imprisonment. He had put his face between two of the bars in order to look out, when he suddenly heard a rattling noise in the ironwork: a chain that he had often noticed running up from the bars and disappearing into the wall was moving and at that moment, he could feel, from the slow outward give of the bars, that the grille was open and letting him out. He went out and walked about in several parts of the island. He could now have used the opportunity to escape, but because his uncle had freely let him out he didn't use it and so returned voluntarily to his prison. As he approached the grille, it was shut but it opened as he came up and let him in, closing behind him again.

All these things would have softened Victor's heart, if the man had not earlier touched his heart most nearly by letting him free his dog.

As a consequence, the young man began for his part to do the same, that is to observe the old man more closely, and often the thought came to him: "Who knows whether he is as hard-hearted as all that, or isn't instead much more likely an unhappy old man."

And so the two continued living together, two stems from the same family tree, and who should therefore have been closer to each other than to anyone else but who could not in fact have been further apart—two stems from the same family tree and yet so different: Victor, like all beginnings, free and full of life, his eyes shining softly, a blank sheet for deeds and joys to come—the other man, in sharp decline, with his defeated air and with every feature marked by a bitter past; but it was this same past that at the time he had seized hold of both for his pleasure and, as he had thought, his profit. In the whole house there lived but four people: his uncle, old Christopher, Rosalie—that was the name of the old housekeeper and cook—and lastly the dim-witted Agnes, who was Rosalie's drudge. It was amongst these old people and between these old walls that Victor walked about like a fish on dry land. Even the dogs were old; the fruit trees growing there were old, the stone dwarves, the wooden beams in the boathouse—they were all old! Victor had only one companion who, like him, was in bloom, and that was the whole plant world, the trees, bushes and flowers, which burgeoned and sprouted vigorously in the midst of this decay.

There was one matter which gave Victor pause for thought and which had occupied him often before. He did not know, namely, where his uncle's bedroom was, and was unable to discover this, however watchful he was. The thought came to him therefore that this might even have been deliberately concealed out of mistrust. Once, when the young man happened to be passing the stairs down to the kitchen, he overheard the house-keeper saying: "He doesn't trust a soul; how then could he be persuaded to take anyone from Hul into his service? He won't do it. That's why he shaves *himself* so that no one can cut his throat, and why he locks up the dogs at night so they won't gobble him up while he's asleep!"

Victor now found himself constantly dwelling on such signs of extreme helplessness on his uncle's part, the more especially so just now, when he was experiencing a softening in his unfavourable disposition towards him. The iron-trellised door in the corridor that led to his bedroom was no longer locked; the wooden gate was regularly open during swimming hours; and his uncle had given him, instead of a key, a whistle for the main grille in the perimeter wall—when he blew on this, the grille opened, since it could not normally be locked or opened except by means of a device operated from one of his uncle's rooms, the only thing being that no one knew which room it was.

The first proper conversations between the two relations came about in a strange fashion—one might say that envy was the cue. It happened one evening when Victor returned from a trek round the island, something he often did now, accompanied by all four dogs, his uncle's included, for these had taken to following him around for a while now and had become livelier and more high-spirited in his and his dog's company than they had formerly been. It was on seeing this that his uncle, who happened to be still in the garden, said: "Your Pomeranian is a far better specimen than my three creatures—they're not to be trusted. I can't understand what makes them so keen on you."

At this, and because he felt it so strongly, the boy instantly replied: "Be affectionate with them like I am with mine and they'll be as good, too."

The man gave him a strangely searching look and said nothing more on the subject. But this became the anchor to which, in the evenings at table, other conversations on other topics were linked. And so things continued thus and uncle and nephew now spoke to each other again whenever they were together, which was the case at the three mealtimes in fact.

Victor became particularly lively on one occasion when the old man, by chance or intentionally, got him to speak about his future and his plans. He would now be taking up his post, Victor said, would be working as hard as he could, improving every shortcoming he came across, putting forward to his superiors everything that could be changed, not tolerating any lounging about and any malpractice—in his free time he would take up the study of the sciences and languages of Europe, so as to prepare himself for future literary work; then he wanted to learn about the business of war, too, in order to have a complete picture of how things worked once he was in the upper echelons of the civil service, or in order, in times of danger, to be fit to serve his country, even as a general. If, furthermore, his talents could extend to it, he would also not want to neglect the muses totally, but see whether he might not succeed in producing something that could enthuse and rouse his countrymen.

During this speech his uncle had been rolling little balls of bread and had listened, smiling with his thin, pinched lips.

"Let's hope you can pull it all off," he said. "At the moment you can swim well, that is, quite well. I watched you again yesterday for a while—but the arc you make with your right arm still comes a little short, as if you were holding your hand back, and also you still move your feet too vigorously. Wouldn't you like to try your hand out at some hunting, too? Do you know how to fire and gun and load it? I'll give you a pair from my gun room and you can take them with you round the whole island."

"Yes, of course I know how to handle a gun," Victor replied, "but I don't want to shoot the songbirds I see here, for I feel too sorry for them and on the whole island I can see only ancient old fruit trees grown over with woodland vegetation, so there's unlikely to be any fox or other game for the shooting."

"You'll find it all right, you just have to know about how to track them."

So saying, his uncle emptied his wine glass, ate his dessert and let the matter drop. After this they soon went off to bed. Victor was no longer taken to his sleeping quarters by his uncle, as in the early days, but, ever since the grille door to his rooms was no longer locked, he would light a candle at the end of the meal, wish his uncle a goodnight and head off for his rooms with his dog, who now ate peaceably with the other dogs.

It was under these circumstances that the time Victor had in fact been forced into agreeing to spend on the island finally came to an end. He was never tempted to say anything about this matter as he was too proud. But when the last day had passed when it was still possible to be there and yet be on time to take up his post, his heart was in his mouth. The evening meal was over. His uncle had left the table and was rummaging about among a number of different bits of paper, clumsily shoving them here and there, as old people do. But then he put everything down in one corner and left it all lying there. Victor could see clearly from his whole behaviour that the old man didn't want to say anything more about the matter, so he took up his light and headed for bed.

The next day breakfast was eaten at the same slow pace as ever. Victor had packed his knapsack in his room and now sat over his breakfast, waiting to hear what his uncle would begin by saying. The old man, who was dressed in his loosely-fitting grey coat, stood up and went in and out of the concealed door a couple of times. Then he said to Victor: "When do you want to be off, today or tomorrow?"

"It must be today, uncle, if I'm not to get there too late," Victor replied.

"Over there in Attmaning you'll be able to get transport."

"I had already reckoned with that and that's definitely what I'll have to do now," said Victor, "for since you didn't mention it at all, I've waited till the last minute."

"So you must go today," the old man said hesitatingly, "you must … well, if you must, then Christoph will have to take you across, as I said. Have you put all your belongings together?"

"I packed everything yesterday."

"Yesterday already—and so you must be really looking forward—well, well! But there was something more I wanted to say to you … what was it? Listen, Victor!"

"Yes, uncle?"

"I think … I believe … if you were now to try, if you would now of your own free will stay a little longer with an old man who has no one."

"How can I, though?"

"I thought I had your leave of absence there—wait a moment, in the pipe table—I thought I put it there."

So saying, his uncle now opened and closed several

drawers of the table and cupboard on which the pipes and pouches were, until he pulled a piece of paper out of one of them and handed it to Victor.

"There you are."

The young man was greatly astonished and embarrassed for the paper was indeed a leave of absence with no date specified.

"You can do as you please now," his uncle said. "I can have you taken across immediately—but I've asked you to stay here a short while longer, to see if we might get along living together. Meanwhile you can go over to Hul or wherever else you want, and when you finally want to leave, then you can."

Victor was nonplussed. He had waited a long time for this day—he now looked at this strange man he actually hated, standing there in front of him, and asking something of him. He found his old, wizened face unutterably forlorn—indeed he even had the impression that some kind of feeling might be trembling within. The boy had always had a good, gentle heart and this now stirred in him. He stood there for a moment only and then, with his characteristic frankness, said: "I'm happy to stay a while longer, uncle, if you wish it, if on examination you deem it right and have your reasons."

"I have no other reason other than wanting you to be here a little longer," the old man said.

He then picked up from the table the paper containing the leave of absence and put it, after first trying three drawers, into a fourth one, in which there was collection of stones.

Victor, who had left his room that morning having no inkling that matters would take such a turn, returned there and slowly unpacked his knapsack. He was now doubly uncertain and doubly intrigued as to where all this was heading and what had led to his uncle to go to such special lengths as to procure leave for him before he had even taken up his post. For a moment there flashed through his mind the question: was it affection—would the man in fact prefer in the end a living human being to the dead and inert profusion of objects and clutter with which he surrounded himself? But then he remembered how nonchalantly the old man had taken the piece of paper from the table and looked for a drawer he could hide it away in. Victor had for some time made the general observation that his uncle never put a thing back in the same place but always in a new one. And while he'd been hunting about, he had not given the young man a second glance but let him leave without saying anything to him.

And so he stayed.

His uncle had a library in the house but he hadn't read anything for a long while, as a result of which the various works had dust and moths in them. He gave Victor the key to this room and this pleased the boy greatly. He had never seen a collection of books, apart from the public ones in town, in which, however, he was understandably not allowed to rummage freely. He made a note of the passageway and often went into this room. He put the ladder against all the shelves and first he cleaned all the books and then read and looked at those that came to hand and which drew his attention.

It also afforded him great pleasure to be able to jump down into the lake by going into the upper floor of the boathouse and out of the door from which his uncle had watched him. The purpose of the door and upper floor had been to enable the monks to unload straight away from the boat those things that would otherwise have been too heavy to take up the steps. And he did after all select a beautiful old German gun from his uncle's gun cabinet, enjoyed cleaning it and then, despite its unwieldiness, firing it. These gunshots, stirring the mountain echoes into life, must have been the first heard on the island for many a long while. Christoph had shown the boy a dark passageway, through which you could go directly from the old man's house across into the cloister. He had also unlocked for him many rooms that were otherwise always closed. He showed him the large hall in which there were gold mouldings and embellishments, where the painted windows glowed white, grey and blue, where long wooden benches, at which the monks had sat, ran the length of the wall and where an unusually large oven stood, each tile of which held colour-enamelled portraits and stories of the saints. He showed him the chapter house, where the monks would confer and where now only the plain, rough wooden benches stood and where a few worthless pictures were hanging, which had been left behind. He showed him the empty treasury room, he showed him the sacristy, where the cupboards for the chalices now stood open, revealing nothing but the threadbare and once dark-red lining, and where the drawers in which once the vestments had been kept and which now contained dust. They went back through the church, the cloisters and the abbot's summer residence, where, untouched, many fine pictures were still hanging and where wood and stone decorative work stood out, since the value of these works had not been recognised when the rest had been taken out of this house of God.

It wasn't only in the buildings and over the whole island that Victor was allowed to wander round and explore but his uncle also offered to have him taken in a boat to any part of the lake he wanted. The young man made little use of this offer because, never having been in mountain country before, he didn't actually know how best to unearth its treasures so as to enjoy and profit from the experience. He went over on his own just twice to Mount Orla and stood on the shore, looking at the high grey rock faces, with the light flashing sporadically on them.

Despite everything Victor gradually began to regret staying there, and in particular because he was not able to fathom the purpose and reason for the whole business.

"I'll be letting you go soon," his uncle said one day after lunch, just as a magnificent storm was crossing over Mount Grisel and noisily pelting down rain like diamond bullets into the lake, so that the water stirred and seethed in small upward spurts. It was because of this storm that they had lingered a little longer at table.

Victor made no reply but listened to hear what would follow.

"It's all futile at the end of the day," his uncle began again, speaking slowly, "it's all futile—youth and old age don't mix. Look at you—you're fine enough—firm and upright, and you amount to more than your father did at the same age. I've watched you for some time and you're someone who might perhaps be relied on. You have a naturally strong and fine-looking physique, and you enjoy employing your strength, whether it's walking around under the cliffs, or in the open air, or swimming in the water—but what's the use of all that? For me it's a blessing that time and space have put far, far beyond my reach. Always I've heard this secret voice saying: you won't get him to look at you, you won't win his heart because it's a treasure you didn't sow, didn't plant. And that is the case, I know it. The years that might have been used for that are over now, they're setting beyond the mountains and there's no power that can drag them over to this side where the cold shadows are lying already. So go to the old woman—you can hardly expect a letter from her now—go and be happy and cheerful."

Victor was deeply affected. The old man was sitting there in such a way that the flashes of lightning lit up his face, and sometimes in the dimly-lit room it seemed as if fire were flowing through the man's grey hair and a rippling light were passing across his weather-worn face. If before the young man had found the empty silences and cold indifference bleak and disturbing, he was now all the more moved by this excited outburst. The old man had sat up tall and straight in the armchair and come near to showing deep emotion. For a while the youth gave no reply to his uncle's speech, the meaning of which he more guessed at than understood. But then he said: "You spoke of letters, Uncle. I must truly confess it has greatly disturbed me that I have still not had a single reply to the numerous letters I have sent home, even though Christoph has been over in Hul and Attmaning more than twenty times since I have been here."

"I knew it would," his uncle replied, "but you cannot receive a reply."

"Why not?"

"Because that's how I arranged things and agreed with them that they wouldn't write to you for the length of your stay here. In any case, if you are worried, they are all fine and healthy."

"That was not a good thing to do, uncle," Victor said, much affected. "I should have dearly loved to hear what my foster-mother might have written."

"There, you see how much you love the old woman," his uncle said. "I always thought so."

"If you loved someone, then someone would love you," replied Victor.

"I might have loved you," the old man cried out, almost making Victor tremble. There were a few moments of silence.

"And old Christoph loves me," he resumed, " and the old maidservant, too, perhaps."

"Why are you silent, then?" he said to the boy after a while. "What are the chances of love being reciprocated? Say something, will you."

Victor was silent, unable to utter a single word.

"You see," his uncle repeated, "I knew it. But don't worry, everything's all right, it's fine. You want to leave and I'll give you a boat so that you can. You'll wait, though, until the rain has stopped?"

"Yes, and longer if you have something serious you want to say to me," the young man said. "But you must recognise that a person cannot be bound merely by some cold whim. It is certainly strange, to say the very least, how to begin with you held me prisoner on this island you had summoned me to earlier, and to which I came in good faith because you demanded it and because my guardian and mother warmly urged it. It is furthermore strange how you cut off all correspondence from my mother—and what may or may not have gone on earlier I find even stranger."

"You speak from your understanding of things," his uncle replied, looking long at the youth. "There are many things that may appear harsh to you because you fail to grasp their purpose and objective. There's nothing strange about what I did—in fact it is clear and evident. I wanted to see you because you will inherit my money one day and that's why I wanted to see you for a long while. No one gave me a child because parents always want to keep them for themselves; whenever one of my acquaintances died, I moved away somewhere else until I finally came to this island, where I acquired the land along with the house, which was once the monks' courthouse. I wanted to let the grass and trees here grow as they have done, so that I could wander about among them. I wanted to see you. I wanted to see your eyes, your hair, your limbs and how else you were fashioned, just as one might a son. I therefore had to have and keep you alone. If they had written to you all the time, then they'd have kept you in that mawkish dependence you've enjoyed till now. I had to pull you out into the sun and the air, lest you become a soft thing like your father and, like him, so ineffectual that you betray that which you think you love. You have indeed grown stronger than him, you lunge forward with your claws like a young hawk—that's good and I applaud you for it but you should test your mettle not with soft-hearted women but at the hard rock face— and I'm closer to being a rock face than anything else. Keeping you here was necessary: whoever cannot now and then apply brute force to the block of stone will also never be capable of working the virgin soil and being of use in the world. You sometimes show your teeth but you have a good heart. That's as it should be. In the end you would have become a son—you would have been moved to respect and love me—and if you had done that, then the others, who have also never been able to get to the core of me, would have appeared tame and small fry to you. But I have come to see that it would take a hundred years for you to get that far, so you should go wherever you want now—it's all over. How many times I asked them to send you, before they finally did! Your father should have given you to *me*—but he said I was a beast of prey that would rip you apart; I would instead have turned you into an eagle that held the world in its talons, one that, if need be, would have thrown it into the abyss, too. But first he loved the woman, then he left her but wasn't strong enough to keep her away permanently, and so thought about her constantly and, when he died, put you under her wing where you would have become little better than a hen, fit only for clucking for its chicks and for squawking if one were trampled under a horse's hoof. Just in these few weeks with me here you have become more than that, because you've had to struggle against force and oppression, and so you would have continued. I demanded that you made your way here on foot so that you would come to know a little about the open air, bodily fatigue, self-mastery. I did what I could after the death of your father, Hippolite—you'll hear about that soon. I had you come to me so that, along with other things you need to learn, I could give you the kind of good advice that neither that pen-pusher, your guardian, nor the woman can give you, and which you can either follow or not, as you please. Since you want to leave today already perhaps, but certainly tomorrow, I want to give you that advice. Listen, then. Is it then your plan to take up a post which they have arranged for you and which will earn you your daily bread and provide for your needs?"

"Yes, uncle."

"Look, I've already procured one period of leave for you. How much must they need you and how important must the post be that can remain waiting for you unfilled? I have here a grant of leave for an unspecified period. At any time I can obtain your resignation as soon as I want. The post, therefore, doesn't require your own particular abilities—in fact there's already someone in the wings, waiting for the position once you've stepped down. You

131

also don't yet in fact have any of the skills that would really be of use when taking up a position, since you're barely out of childhood and have so far had only the tiniest corner of this earth to learn something from—and still don't know that even. So if you were to take up the post now, you would, at the most, be able to do something which would profit no one but which would slowly grind the life out of you. But there's another way for you I have in mind. The greatest and most important thing you have to to do now is this: you must marry."

Victor turned his clear gaze to him and asked: "What?!"

"You must marry—not immediately of course but while you're young. I'll tell you why. Everyone is out for himself. Not everyone will say so but everyone *behaves* so. And those that don't say so often behave in an even more grossly selfish way. And those who devote themselves to an employment know this only too well, for their job is for them the field that is meant to yield them fruit. Everyone is out for what they can get for themselves but not everyone can get what they want and there is many a man who ekes out his life for less than a pittance. The man put in charge of your protection thought he was looking after you well by cooping up your young life with the sole aim of your always being able to eat and drink your fill; the woman, out of the goodness of her heart, scraped together a small sum—I even know precisely how much—a small sum that will enable you to keep yourself in hose for a while. She meant well by it, the best of intentions, for she has the best will in the world. But what's the point of it all? Every man is out for himself but he only makes something of this life when all the strengths granted him are set to work and activated—for that is what living and what pleasure are—and when he thus drinks this cup of life dry. And as soon as he is strong enough to give full rein to his powers—all of them, mind, both great and small—it is then that he is best placed to be of service to others, too, as indeed he always was. For we cannot avoid affecting those around us, since compassion, sympathy, readiness to help, these, too, are powers requiring to be called into action. I'd even say that devoting oneself to others—even unto death—is nothing less than the flower of a man's life, bursting open in its finest form. But the man who in his poverty harnesses only one strength in order to satisfy just one single demand, that of hunger, perhaps, that is a one-sided and wretched madness, damaging both for the man himself, and for those who come within his circle. Oh, Victor, what do you know of life? What do you know of what they call old age?"

"How should I, uncle, being still so young?"

"Yes, it's true—you don't, nor can you either. Life is immeasurably long while you are still young. You always think there's so much ahead of you and that you've only gone a short way. And so you postpone things, put this and that to one side to be taken up later. But when you do want to take it up it's too late and you realise you're old. That's why life seems a vast expanse when viewed from the beginning but scarcely a stone's throw when at the end you look back over your shoulder. And so many a fruit ripens there that you didn't know you'd planted. It's a dazzling sight at first, so beautiful you want to plunge into it, believing it must last for ever—and old age is a moth at dusk fluttering about one's ears, chilling the heart. And so you want to reach out your hands so as to cling on because there's so much you have missed. When an ancient old man stands on top of a hill made up of a whole welter of his life's deeds, what good is that to him? I have done many and various things and have nothing to show for them. Everything falls apart in a moment if you haven't created a life that lasts beyond the grave. That man around whom, in his old age, sons, grandsons and great-grandsons stand will often live to be a thousand. There is a diversity of life there but of the same stamp and when he is gone, then that same life continues—indeed you don't even notice that a small part of that life has stepped to one side and is no longer there. At my death everything that I have been, that I am, will perish ... which is why you must marry, Victor, marry very young. And that is why you must also have enough breathing space for you to be able to stretch all your limbs, and I have taken care of this because I knew that none of those to whom you were entrusted were capable of it. After your father's death any authority I had was taken from me and yet I have taken better care of things than the others. I set about rescuing the property that you otherwise would have lost. Don't look so amazed, just listen. What good to you are your mother's little savings or the lifetime of labour your guardian arranged? Good for nothing more than to break and stunt you.

I have been miserly but more sensibly so than many
another is generous, who throws away his money and
then can help neither himself nor others. While he was
alive I lent your father small sums, as brothers otherwise
make over as gifts; he gave me receipts for these, which
I had registered as charges on his estate. When he then
died and the other creditors who had inveigled him came
to plunder the wretched nest, I was there before them
and, exercising my rights, snatched it from them and
from your guardian, who also wanted to claim a small
remnant on your behalf. How short-sighted they were! I
slowly repaid the creditors what they had advanced along
with the interest, but not what they had been hoping
to scavenge. The estate is now free of debt and fifteen
years' worth of proceeds is sitting in the bank for you.
Tomorrow before you go I'll give you the papers, for now
that I have said everything it's best you go. I have sent
Christoph over to Hul to get the fisherman who brought
you to fetch you again tomorrow from the landing place,
for Christoph doesn't have time to take you over himself.
Should you not want to travel tomorrow but later, then
we can give the fisherman his fare and have him go back
again empty. I think you should go into farming, as the
ancient Romans were happy to do; they well knew how
to set about things so that all one's abilities are properly
and uniformly employed. But in any event you can do
what you want. Enjoy what you have in your own fashion. If you are wise, that's good; if you are a fool, then
in your old age you can rue your life, as I have rued
mine. I have done much that was good, I have had much

135

pleasure from life and from what it rightly gives us to enjoy—that was good, but there is much I have neglected to do and that has led me to regret and mull over these things, both of which are futile. For life flew by before I could seize hold of it. You are probably my heir, too, and so I want you to do better than I have done. Hence my advice—and I say 'advice' not condition, since no one should be bound to anything. Go travelling now for two to three years, then come back and marry; to begin with, keep the manager of your estate I appointed, for he will give you sound guidance. That is my opinion but do what you will."

The old man said nothing after this. He folded his napkin together as usual, rolled it up and pushed it thus through the silver ring he had for this purpose. He then put the various bottles together in a certain order, placed the cheese and confectionery on their plates, covering these with their appropriate glass lids. But he didn't carry any of these things from the table, as he always did normally, but left them standing there and remained seated. The storm meanwhile had moved on, the flashes of lightning growing fainter, the rolls of thunder weaker, as it passed down to the other side of the eastern peaks; the sun emerged again after a struggle, filling the room slowly with a loving glow. Victor was sitting opposite his uncle, shocked and unable to speak.

After a considerable while, the old man, who had been sitting there in front of his things all the time, began to speak again, and said: "If you already have a prefer-ence for a young woman, that doesn't matter as regards marrying—it's not an obstacle and often no help either, so take her; but if you don't have such a preference, then that is of no consequence either, for such things are not constant, they come and they pass, whether you seek them out or repel them. I experienced such a feeling once—as you'll have probably heard—and while on the subject I'll show you the picture I had painted of her, how she looked then—wait, perhaps I can find it."

At this the old man stood up and looked around in his chests of drawers, first in this room, then in another, but he couldn't find the picture. Finally he pulled it out of a drawer by its dusty gold chain. He wiped the glass with the sleeve of his grey coat, handed it to Victor and said: "There, you see!"

Victor, however, blushed crimson and cried: "That's Hanna, my sister."

"No," said his uncle, "it's Ludmilla, her mother. How can you think it's Hanna? The picture was painted long before she was born. Did your foster-mother tell you nothing about me, then?"

"Yes, she did. She told me you were my uncle and that you lived in great seclusion on the island of a distant mountain lake."

"She thinks I'm the most terrible villain."

"No, uncle, she doesn't. She has never spoken ill of anyone and when she spoke of you she always gave us to understand that you travelled the world a lot, that you'd grown old and now lived very much alone and cut off from the world, every corner of which you had earlier enjoyed visiting."

"And she said nothing else about me?"

"No, uncle, nothing."

"Hm—that is good of her. I might have realised. If only she had been but a little stronger and the clear understanding she possessed had been able to encompass a wider world—then everything would have been different. And she said nothing, too, about my wanting to rob you of your little property?"

"Never anything about robbing, just that you have the rights to it."

"That's true, but already in my youth I was very active, started off in commerce, extended my business activities and made more money than I'll ever need, and so have no need at all of that little property."

"My foster-mother also always insisted in the past that I should come to you as you wished, but my guardian prevented it."

"There, you see!—Your guardian means well in all respects but the table at which he sits blinds him to the world, to the sea, to everything. He thought perhaps that with me you'd forget some of the things which you've learnt and which, as far as the rest of your life is concerned, are of no value. I once wanted to make your foster-mother my wife, as you see; she won't have told you that either?"

"No, she didn't and neither did my guardian."

"We were very young, she was vain and I said I wanted to have her portrait painted. She agreed and the artist, who came with me from the town, painted her on this oval ivory plaque. I kept the portrait and later had the gold circular edging added and the gold chain made for it. I was very attached to her then and showed her many tokens of my affection. At that time I used to go on my travels in order get to know my business partners and to set up new business ventures and connections, and whenever I returned home from these I would be very attentive and also bring her back many a very beautiful present. She didn't return my attentions, however; she was friendly but didn't show any affection and didn't say why; she wouldn't accept my gifts, giving me no reason for this either. When I finally came straight out with it and declared that I would be happy to make her my wife without further ado, if she was willing, now or perhaps later, she replied that she was indeed honoured but was unable to feel the kind of affection that seemed to her necessary for a lifelong union. When after some time I went up to the beech-forest spring in Hirschkar, I saw her sitting on the large stone slab near the spring. Her shawl, which she liked to wear about her shoulders on cooler days, was hanging on the level branch of a beech tree that was set back a bit; the branch was not high off the ground and reached out from the tree, just like a rod for hanging things on. Her hat was likewise next to the shawl. Sitting with her on the stone, however, was my brother, Hippolit, and they were holding each other in a close embrace. This had long been the spot where they had their rendezvous, something I only found out much later. At first I wanted to murder him, but then I tore down the shawl that concealed me like a curtain and cried: 'It would be better in the end if you did everything openly and married each other.' From that day on I began to put his property in order and to further his career so that they might have each other. But when later your father had to leave to go elsewhere for a time in order to promote his career even further, he felt duty-bound, once there, to denounce a fatherly friend who, temporarily embarrassed, was making use of office funds. This was already being whispered about in town, and the old man was on the verge of killing himself; your father went to him hurriedly at night, settled the money and, to scotch the rumours, asked for the hand of the man's daughter in marriage, the woman who was later your mother. When the union in fact took place, I then went to Ludmilla and scornfully pointed out to her how incapable she was of using her intelligence and her heart. She moved out to the small holding where she now lives with the man she later married. But these are all old stories, Victor, they all took place a long, long time ago and have faded away from people's memories."

He had been sitting in his armchair again while thus speaking and now he picked the picture up from the table where he had set it down, stood up, wound it in the chain and put it in a little drawer next to his pipe collection.

The storm meanwhile had blown itself out completely, apart from the odd bits of mist and cloud, which, as happens in such cases, were still gathering in the valley; these alternately either veiled or were pierced through by the sun, which had been raying down warmly for some while now.

Whenever the old man had once got up from eating, it wasn't easy for him to sit down again. This was the case now, too. He took his bottles from the table, put them in the wall cupboards and locked them away. He dealt similarly with the cheese and confectionery and took the precaution of pouring the dogs some water into their trough.

When he had done all this he went to the window and looked down into the garden.

"Do you see," he said to Victor, "it's just like I told you recently. The sand is almost dry and in an hour's time you'll be able to walk around on it very easily. That's the quartz soil here: it lightly covers the rocky ground and has this quality of absorbing downpours like a sieve. That's why I always have to add so much humus for the flowers and why so many of the monks' fruit trees tend to die, whereas the elms, oaks, beech and the other mountain trees here flourish, because they seek out the rock, force open cracks in it and burrow their way in."

Victor also went over to the window and looked down.

Later, when the housekeeper came and cleared the table, and when Christoph, who was back from Hul already, led the dogs out, the old man went through the concealed door into the gun room.

The boy, however, who would in fact have wandered about in the open far and wide after the storm, now went to his room and stood at the window staring out …

After a while he saw his uncle down in the garden tying flowers to small stakes.

After walking up and down in his room a while longer,

he finally left it after all and went outside again. He walked across the sandy forecourt—his uncle was no longer there—and towards the lakeshore where there was a rocky ridge forming an elevated spot, which offered a remarkable panorama. There he stopped and looked out. Meanwhile evening had set in. Some of the mountains lay in the embrace of dark wisps of cloud, others towered up like glowing coals from the debris, and islands of pale sky shimmered unseen above the boy's head. He gazed out at this picture until gradually everything burnt out and was extinguished, and there was nothing there any more save thick darkness.

Through this darkness he then walked slowly and pensively past the black ghosts of the trees and back into the house.

He had decided to leave the island the next day.

When it was time for dinner he made his way out of his room and along the passage into the dining-room. His uncle was already seated at table and straight away dinner was served. The old man informed the youth that Christoph had brought back the news from Hul that the fisherman would be waiting for him at the landing place where he had set Victor down on his arrival.

"So you can leave tomorrow after breakfast," his uncle concluded, "if that's what you have resolved to do, for you are completely your own master and can do what you please."

"I have indeed made up my mind to set off tomorrow," Victor replied, "but I place the matter in your hands, uncle, and will do whatever you think best."

"If that's the case," his uncle said, "then I think it best, as I said at midday, that you go tomorrow. Whatever will be, will be, and as you wish to follow my advice, then follow it. You are in every respect at liberty."

"Then I'll look out for the fisherman tomorrow at the landing place," replied Victor.

These words were the only ones the two relatives spoke during the meal concerning their relations with one another. They went on to speak about several other matters. In particular, his uncle told him that old Christoph had gone over to Hul before the storm, where it had had a devastating effect, especially at the mouth of the Afel, that the landslide had brought down fresh and indeed huge amounts of rubble and that the water had burst its banks in a dreadful fashion.

"And here, as it passed over the Grisel," he continued, "it was so gentle and tame that it watered my flowers for me, knocking hardly any of their stems over. Christoph, when he crossed back over after the storm, was surprised to find such little devastation here."

When dinner was over the two relatives wished each other a last goodnight and repaired to bed, except that Victor still had to pack his knapsack, this time not in vain, he thought, and then he laid out his travelling clothes on a chair.

When the next day dawned, he dressed in these clothes, took up his travelling staff and hung his knapsack over his arm by one of the straps. His dog, who understood everything, danced for joy.

Over breakfast little of any import was said.

"I'll come with you as far as the gate," his uncle said, when Victor had stood up, put his knapsack on his back and showed signs of wanting to take his leave.

The old man had gone into the neighbouring room and must have pressed a spring or closed some other device for in that moment Victor heard the clanking of the gate and through the window saw it slowly opening.

"So," his uncle said, as he came back in, "all set."

Victor fetched his staff and put on his hat. The old man went down the steps with him, across the garden and as far as the gate. On the way neither said a word. At the gate his uncle stopped, drew a small bundle from his pocket and said: "Here are the papers."

However, Victor replied: "I'd rather not take them, uncle, if you'll allow."

"What? Not take them? What are you thinking of?"

"Please. And don't do my feelings a violence," Victor said, "but let me do things my way in this, so that you can see I am not self-seeking."

"I'll not force you," the old man said, and pushed his papers back in his pocket.

Victor looked at him for a moment. The tears glistened as they filled his bright eyes, testimony of his deep feelings—then he bent down suddenly and fervently kissed his uncle's wrinkled hand.

The old man let out a strange, muffled sound—like a sob—and pushed the youth out through the gate.

Immediately the clattering noise could be heard and the clank as the gate closed and the lock snapped shut. Victor turned round and saw the old man's back in its grey coat, as he walked towards his house. The young man pressed his handkerchief to his eyes, which were streaming in torrents that would not cease. Then he, too, turned back again and started out on the way that led to the place where he had first set foot on this island. He walked down one side of the hollow and up the other, through the dwarf garden, through the little wood with its tall trees and through the thicket. When he came to the landing place, his eyes had dried but were still a little reddened. The old man from Hul was waiting for him there already, as well as the friendly, blue-eyed girl, who was standing in the stern of the boat. Victor climbed in with his dog and sat down. Immediately the boat was pushed out, while its prow swung round so it faced the lake and then plunged forward into the lake water, while the island behind retreated.

When they reached the headland beneath Mount Orla, the island was already a long way behind and, as before, reared up with its green trees out of the water. As the body of the boat now made the turn round the mountain base, so the headland began to cover up the island, making it appear like a green tongue, which on the journey there had grown ever longer but which now withdrew behind the mountain walls. At last, as they approached Hul, only the blue walls encircling and reflected in the solitary water were visible, just as when Victor had first set off.

In Hul Victor tarried a short while, in order to talk with the fisherman and give him his fare. No mention was made, however, of the tales of old that had been the subject on the outward journey.

When he had landed in Hul, he had already seen the ravages of yesterday's storm from the furrowed-up ground and the damage done to the shore. The landslide, however, had left a horrific amount of debris lying about, this having fallen down from high up, loosened by the eroding effect of the water. From this scene of devastation he walked on towards the mouth of the river Afel and from there up through the long forest path.

On the ridge he stopped and looked back at the lake. Mount Grisel could barely be seen, but the bare and darkening rock face he had so admired when he first arrived was Mount Orla. He looked at this now for a while and thought to himself that behind there was the island, where things would now be as so often they had been when he had come back from his long walks—back from the fluttering sycamores, back from the rush of the surf—that somewhere on it two lonely old men were sitting, one here, the other there, with neither of them speaking to the other.

Two hours later he was in Attmaning and, as he emerged out of the dark trees and walked towards the town, he happened to hear the ringing of the town's bells, and never had a sound seemed to him so sweet as this ringing, which thrilled his ear because he had not heard it for so long. In the street outside the inn were cattle merchants with their beautiful brown mountain breed, which they were driving down to the plains, and the inn itself was packed with people, since it was the weekly market. It seemed to Victor that he had been dreaming for a long time and now was back in the world.

After he had eaten his meal at this inn where the land-lord had earlier lent him the young lad, he set off on the further stage of his journey, not with the lad this time, but in the landlord's fine little wagon, which took him trundling alongside the course of the Afel and into more open country.

When he came once again to the fields of men, to roads and the lively bustle of fellow human beings—when the land, set off with gentle hills, spread out endlessly far and wide in front of him and the forsaken mountains hovered behind him like a blue wreath, then, on seeing this vast panorama, his heart took wing and hurried him far, far over that distant line of the horizon, behind which he was certain his foster-mother and her daughter Hanna lived, the two people he loved above all else.

VI

RETURN

VICTOR GOT DOWN from the hired wagon after a while, since he felt walking was far more pleasant, and set out on the rest of the journey on foot, as before. The long road home to his mother was taken also with the object of asking her, too, the person he so looked up to and loved, for her advice as to what to do next in this new state of affairs. And so it was that after many days spent on this road, walking with his dog through fields and woods, over hill and down dale, he found himself walking again across the shining meadows he had walked over with his friends so many weeks before, and down into his home valley. He walked over the first footbridge, he walked over the second, past the big elder tree and in through the little old garden gate. When he got nearer to the house, he saw his mother standing on the path in front of the apple tree in the clean white pinafore she usually had on in the mornings when she had to attend to things in the kitchen and to the whole round of housework.

"Mother," he cried, "I've brought Pom back to you—he's been well cared for and looked after—and I'm back, too, as I've got a lot to talk to you about."

"Oh, Victor, it's you," cried the old woman. "Welcome, my son, a thousand times welcome, dear child."

So saying, she went towards him, pushed the cap back a little that he had on, stroked his forehead and hair with one hand, while with the other she took his right hand and kissed him on the forehead and cheek.

The dog, who had shot ahead towards the house from the garden gate, now pranced around Victor's mother, barking furiously.

The windows and doors of the house were open, as was usually the case on fine days, so that Hanna, on hearing this racket from inside the house, came running out of the house but then came to a sudden standstill, unable to utter a word.

"So, greet each other, children, greet each other, after being apart for the very first time."

Victor walked closer and said shyly: "Hello, dear Hanna."

"Hello to you, dear Victor," she replied, taking his outstretched hand.

"And now go inside, children," their mother said. "Victor has to set down his things and say what he needs, whether he's tired perhaps and what we can give him to eat."

So saying, she made to go inside, taking the children, as she called them, with her. In the big room Victor put his knapsack down by the table he hadn't expected to see again so soon, leant his staff in a corner and sat down on a chair. His mother sat down in the large armchair next to him.

The dog, because he had become, as it were, so important and belonged to the new arrival, went in with them, but when they had begun to talk and exchange news, he went out again and because he could clearly see that all danger now of his being separated from his friend, Victor, had disappeared, he was seen later lying in his kennel under the apple tree, comfortably sleeping off the tiredness he had accumulated in the course of all the travels he had undergone.

Being seated at the table, Victor's mother urged him to say whether he was hungry, whether he needed anything else, and that he should feel free to do anything that would help him recuperate. He answered that he didn't need anything, that he wasn't tired, that he had break-fasted late and could therefore wait until the usual time for the midday meal, and after she had eventually gone out in order to make arrangements for a more sufficient and better meal, she then came back in again, sat down where he was and began to speak about his affairs.

"Victor," she said, "when you had been away for sever-al days, a letter from your uncle came, in which he asked us not to write to you for the whole period while you were with him. I assumed he must have a reason for making such a demand, that he perhaps he had something in mind that would prove useful to you, and so I agreed. You will have felt really hurt when you didn't hear a sin-gle syllable from us, no greeting, no friendly word."

"Mother, my uncle is a wonderful, excellent man," Victor interjected.

"Yesterday another letter arrived from him addressed to your guardian with all sorts of documents," said his mother. "Your guardian drove out here and read the letter out to us. Your uncle thought that you would probably be back home and wanted you to be told of the letter. Now you must hear what it contains. Yes, he is an excellent man, no one can know that better than I, which is why

I always insisted you should be allowed to go to him, as he demanded, until your guardian agreed. But Victor my dear, he also has a rough and hard side, which is why he has never been able to get anyone to love him. Many is the time I was reminded by him of the saying in the Holy Scriptures about how the Divine Form would appear one day, not in the rolling of the thunder, not in the roaring of the storm but in the rustling of the breeze moving alongside the stream and through the fruit-laden bushes. I had no idea then, when we were all still young, that I would find myself obliged to regard him highly. One day when you're older, I will tell you something about us."

"He told me about it himself, mother,"

"He told you himself, child?" the old woman answered. "Then he's been better disposed to you than I thought."

"He just briefly told me the facts."

"I'll tell them to you one day at greater length, then you'll see what sorrowful and sad times I went through before everything became so pleasant and beautifully autumnal for me, as it now is. Then you'll also see why it is that I love you so, my poor dear Victor!"

So saying, she put her arm round his head, as old people do, drew him to her a little nearer and laid her cheek against his hair, appearing deeply moved.

When she had gathered herself once more and leant back, she said: "In the letter, Victor, he wrote of what he spoke to you about recently and about what he's done for you."

When her mother said this, Hanna quickly went out of the room.

"He sent the papers," his mother continued, "which transfer the estate to you, to your guardian; you should accept this joyfully and gratefully."

"It's difficult, mother, it's so strange … "

"Your guardian says you should carry out everything exactly as your uncle wishes. You no longer need now to take up the post he wished to set you up in, for this turn of events couldn't have been foreseen and a wonderful life has opened up in front of you."

"But will Hanna be willing?" said Victor.

"Who mentioned Hanna?" replied his mother, her eyes shining with joy.

But Victor was too hotly confused to be able to say anything; he sat there, his cheeks appearing to be about to catch on fire.

"She'll be willing, don't worry," his mother spoke again. "All will be well, child, and everything will turn out for the best. Now we'll be working on all the things you'll be needing for your travels. You are your own master now, a man of means—so everything has to be different and the journey, too, means things must be arranged differently. I'll be taking care of all that. But now I must take care of lunch—go and look round the house meanwhile and see if anything's changed, or do whatever you want—it'll soon be lunchtime anyway."

At these words she got up and went into the kitchen.

When lunch had been prepared and served, the three of them sat again at the table they hadn't sat at together for a long while.

In the afternoon Victor went out for a walk and visited

all the places that had once been dear and familiar to him: Hanna, however, ran around in the house all fingers and thumbs.

In the evening after supper, when he wanted to go to bed and his mother went with him holding a candle, she led him into his old room, and when they entered he saw that nothing had been altered as he had so vividly imagined it would have been when he had set off. Even the suitcase and the boxes were still sitting there where he had packed them.

"You see," his mother said, "we left everything as it was because your uncle wrote that we shouldn't send anything off while it was still uncertain what shape your life would take. And now, goodnight, Victor."

"Good night, mother."

And when she had gone, he looked down through the window at the dark bushes again and the rippling water in which the stars were reflected, and when he was lying in bed he could still hear the rippling of the water, as he had heard it on so many evenings in his childhood and youth.

VII

CONCLUSION

I F WE MAY BE ALLOWED to add something to the scenes of youth represented in the above sections, then it is as follows.

After Victor's mother had finished fitting him out for his journey and everything was settled that could in the future contribute to the well-being of the young man, a farewell took place again in that same year in the middle of autumn. But this time it was not a sad one like the first, since it was not for his whole life, so to speak, but entailed only a short period of necessary absence to be followed by one that would be long, beautiful and rapturous.

The fact that Hanna badly wanted to become a very important part of this happy period was demonstrated by the fiery and passionate kisses with which she covered Victor's lips when they bade each other a private farewell, when he pressed her to him fervently and painfully, declaring himself unable to part from her. The two foster-siblings wept such a deal at this propitious farewell one might have thought it was to divide them, tear them apart in the most dreadful fashion, and not just for a long time but perhaps never allowing hope of a reunion.

Their mother, Ludmilla, however, went about in quiet joyousness, gave her son her blessing on his departure, and wondered constantly how, through the little good she had done in her life—good that she had always wished had been more than it could be—how in her old age she had thus deserved to be so rewarded by God, so greatly, greatly rewarded.

When he was gone, the quiet and simple life in the valley and the house resumed the course it had always followed till then. The old woman went innocently about the business of the house, attending to everything in the best possible way, doing good wherever she was able, and, in view of an approaching event, seeing to the provision and preparation of a wealth of domestic effects and conveniences. Hanna was a devoted daughter, happy at all times to do her mother's will, while waiting excitedly and with a full heart to see what the future would bring.

When four years had passed and the letters from foreign parts all written in the same dear and familiar hand had grown into a very considerable pile, the author himself came and the letters ceased. Victor returned so altered that even his foster-mother was taken aback and surprised, for in this short time, from the almost childish youth, a man had grown. But otherwise only his understanding and mind had developed: the good heart she had laid up in him had remained indestructible, for it was just as childlike and undamaged as it was when she had first given it to him when he was a tender child and then further cultivated, for she had the power to give him her heart, but not what a strong man requires and what the harshness of life demands of him. Hanna saw no change in Victor, for from childhood she had thought him more skilful and capable than herself; the fact that she had a good, simple and great soul disposed to do good as consistently as water flows downhill, this she didn't know, assuming this to be a virtue common to all.

Not very long after his return, Victor stood at the altar with Hanna plighting eternal troth—two creatures whose faces were copies of two others who might also once have been glad to stand before the same altar but who through misfortune and their own fault were torn from each other and then rued it for the rest of their lives.

All the friends who had taken part in that walk to celebrate Ferdinand's birthday were present at this celebration of Victor's and Hanna's. Victor's guardian was also there with his wife, and Rosina, now herself a young wife, and Rosina's and Hanna's childhood friends, and others, too.

When all the celebrations were over, Victor led Hanna in triumph to his estate. Their mother didn't go with them; she said she would see soon enough how everything would turn out.

Victor's uncle had not come to the wedding despite several requests to do so on his nephew's part, who himself had stayed with him. Quite alone he sat on his island, for, as he himself had once said, everything, everything was too late, and something once missed could not be made up for.

If one wished to apply the parable of the barren fig tree to this man, then might one say: the good, gentle Gardener does not cast it into the fire but every spring looks at the barren foliage and, every spring, lets it grow green until even the leaves become fewer and fewer and finally only the dried-up branches stretch upwards.

Then the tree will be taken out of the garden and its place otherwise used. The remaining plants continue, however, to blossom and flourish, but none of these can say that they have sprung from its seed and will bear the sweet fruit that this tree bore. Then the sun continues to shine down, the blue sky smiles from one millennium to the next, the earth clothes itself in its ancient green and the generations descend in a long chain down to the youngest child—but he is obliterated from all this because his life has left no copy of itself, and no offspring of his are numbered are among those carried down the stream of time. Even if, however, he has left other traces of having lived, these too are extinguished—as are all earthly things—and when finally in the ocean of time everything, everything perishes, even the greatest and those things that give most joy, *he* will perish before this moment, because everything in him is already in the throes of swift decline while he still draws breath and while he still lives.

PUSHKIN PRESS

Pushkin Press was founded in 1997, and publishes novels, essays, memoirs, children's books—everything from timeless classics to the urgent and contemporary.

Our books represent exciting, high-quality writing from around the world: we publish some of the twentieth century's most widely acclaimed, brilliant authors such as Stefan Zweig, Marcel Aymé, Teffi, Antal Szerb, Gaito Gazdanov and Yasushi Inoue, as well as compelling and award-winning contemporary writers, including Andrés Neuman, Edith Pearlman, Eka Kurniawan, Ayelet Gundar-Goshen and Chigozie Obioma.

Pushkin Press publishes the world's best stories, to be read and read again. To discover more, visit www.pushkinpress.com.

THE SPECTRE OF ALEXANDER WOLF
GAITO GAZDANOV

'A mesmerising work of literature' Antony Beevor

SUMMER BEFORE THE DARK
VOLKER WEIDERMANN

'For such a slim book to convey with such poignancy the extinction of a generation of "Great Europeans" is a triumph' *Sunday Telegraph*

MESSAGES FROM A LOST WORLD
STEFAN ZWEIG

'At a time of monetary crisis and political disorder… Zweig's celebration of the brotherhood of peoples reminds us that there is another way' *The Nation*

THE EVENINGS
GERARD REVE

'Not only a masterpiece but a cornerstone manqué of modern European literature' Tim Parks, *Guardian*

BINOCULAR VISION

EDITH PEARLMAN

'A genius of the short story' Mark Lawson, *Guardian*

IN THE BEGINNING WAS THE SEA

TOMÁS GONZÁLEZ

'Smoothly intriguing narrative, with its touches of sinister,
Patricia Highsmith-like menace' *Irish Times*

BEWARE OF PITY

STEFAN ZWEIG

'Zweig's fictional masterpiece' *Guardian*

THE ENCOUNTER

PETRU POPESCU

'A book that suggests new ways of looking at the world
and our place within it' *Sunday Telegraph*

WAKE UP, SIR!

JONATHAN AMES

'The novel is extremely funny but it is also sad and
poignant, and almost incredibly clever' *Guardian*

THE WORLD OF YESTERDAY

STEFAN ZWEIG

'*The World of Yesterday* is one of the greatest memoirs of the twentieth
century, as perfect in its evocation of the world Zweig loved, as it is
in its portrayal of how that world was destroyed' David Hare

WAKING LIONS

AYELET GUNDAR-GOSHEN

'A literary thriller that is used as a vehicle to explore big
moral issues. I loved everything about it' *Daily Mail*

FOR A LITTLE WHILE

RICK BASS

'Bass is, hands down, a master of the short form, creating in a few pages
a natural world of mythic proportions' *New York Times Book Review*